Lyn Thompson's eclectic stories are gem-like examinations of human experience which illuminates as much as they entertain with their subtle characterization and deft exposition. *Patchwork Stories* is a treasure trove of the short story writer's craft.

Mark Kirtland
Writer and Editor

Lyn Thompson's short stories are a pleasure to read. They are beautifully written, insightful, and brimming with emotion. A reader will laugh or cry and thoroughly enjoy the journey with her. I was captivated.

Denise LeClaire M.A.
Businesswoman, Reader and Author

From visiting with *ghosts* to being lost in the Canadian wilderness, Lyn Thompson gives the reader fifteen fascinating tales of adventure, intrigue and sometimes whimsy. As with her 2013 story of *Bella, A Woman of Courage,* this is another page-turner.

Susan M.Cameron, M.Ed.
Career Counsellor and Author

PATCHWORK Stories

Lyn Thompson

LYN THOMPSON

PATCHWORK STORIES
Copyright © 2014 by Lyn Thompson

ISBN: 978-1-4866-0607-8

Word Alive Press
131 Cordite Road, Winnipeg, MB R3W 1S1
www.wordalivepress.ca

WORD ALIVE
—P R E S S—

Library and Archives Canada Cataloguing in Publication

Thompson, Lyn, author
    Patchwork stories / Lyn Thompson.

Short stories.
Issued in print and electronic formats.
ISBN 978-1-4866-0607-8 (pbk.).--ISBN 978-1-4866-0608-5 (pdf).--
ISBN 978-1-4866-0609-2 (html).--ISBN 978-1-4866-0610-8 (epub)

        I. Title.

PS8639.H628P37 2014   C813'.6   C2014-905763-6
                                              C2014-905764-4

CONTENTS

I

ANTEBELLUM TIMEPIECE

"This looks like a graveyard! Are you sure this is the right address?" asks Sybil when the taxi pulls up in front of a cemetery with row upon row of crypts and mausoleums.

"Yes, ma'am. This be the right place, but we're on a one-way street. Look across the road. You want the big white house—one of the finest antebellum homes in the city, only it's all apartments now."

A colonnade of white pillars across the front of the home protect a spacious veranda, and an upper balcony makes the house vibrant with history. Gracious landscaping, despite the size of the diminished lot, causes Sybil to pause in awe.

She knows the history of the antebellum home from her Great-Aunt Clara, who lived in the original master bedroom before her unexpected death. The will named Sybil as executor of the estate. She's come to New Orleans to attend to Clara's things and vacate the room before the rent runs out at the end of the month.

While Sybil pays the cab driver, a bright red tour bus parks in front of the taxi, and tourists spill across the boulevard into the cemetery.

"New Orleans has tours of the cemetery?" Sybil asks in disbelief.

"Yes, ma'am," says the taxi driver, "only in N'awlins, we call the cemetery 'The City of the Dead.' With the ocean so close making the water table high, we can't bury people in the ground. We put 'em in one of those tombs, and the hot sun cooks 'em to dust in 'bout a year. The dust falls through the grate to the floor, and the family tomb is ready for another customer. We've got generations of folks in there, and some say we've got ghosts, too. Tourists come here because they like to exercise their imaginations. Go see fo' yo'sef."

The very idea of visiting the cemetery makes Sybil shudder, yet she continues to look across the jumble of family tombs—some granite, some marble. She sees tone on tone of grey, white, black and tan, with a few leafy shrubs showing above the surrounding limestone wall.

As she stands there, sullen clouds wash across the sky. Without sunlight, each crypt speaks only of death. The shiny roof of the cab beads with moisture as the fine mist in the air turns into a light rain. Sybil grabs her suitcase and wheels it over the curb towards the white house. Before passing under the vine-covered portico, Sybil peers through the drizzle at the second floor and wonders which set of windows belong to the master bedroom, Aunt Clara's room.

She rings the bell. A middle-age woman ushers her into a wood-panelled foyer with a green terrazzo floor. An elegant grandfather clock stands sentinel in the curve of the circular staircase. The sway of its brass pendulum marks each passing minute as if ticking away life itself.

After meeting Mrs. Lord, the landlady, Sybil finds herself in Clara's room, standing at the window. Rain drenches the scene below as the City of the Dead rebuffs the tourists. As if in a trance, Sybil wonders how many times Clara stood here communing with long-gone souls. Like it or not, Sybil knows she will venture into the cemetery sooner or later, if only to find the family tomb.

She turns from the window. One sweeping glance of the room tells volumes about Clara's life. A grand four-poster bed boasting an elegant patchwork quilt dominates the room. Off to the right, its matching bureau presides with dignity. At the foot of the bed, Clara's hope chest still waits in vain, as does an opened rolltop desk set near the window. To the right of the door, at the edge of the blue and wine Persian carpet, a little table with two side chairs begs for company—all of it old and shabby like the magnolia-flowered wallpaper and faded rose drapes.

The chimes of the big clock in the lower hall ring six times for supper.

Sybil enters the dining room. Other residents, in groups of two or three, are seated at small tables. The landlady shows Sybil to a table of her own. The dining room radiates with original charm—gas chandeliers now electrified, wainscoting of polished wood, topped with a plate rail, and there against the far wall, a small fireplace. Heads turn and whisper, then sneak another look at the newcomer, but no one speaks to her. She expected her arrival to cause some interest, but somehow she feels that everyone in the room enjoys secrets that will never be shared with an outsider. She wonders why she senses a shadowy aura drifting among them when she knows nothing of auras or extrasensory perception.

3

After supper, Sybil carries her coffee back to Clara's room and sets about examining papers in the desk to rid her thoughts of ghosts and the cemetery. The death certificate claims that Clara died from falling down the circular staircase in the night. Sybil doesn't doubt the story; anything can happen with elderly people. Yet, to Sybil's knowledge, Clara, at seventy-five years, showed no frailty or unsteadiness.

True, thinks Sybil counting on her fingers, *I haven't actually visited with Clara since that summer in Atlanta ten years ago. At that time, Clara declared that I looked just like her at age twenty-five. Maybe that's why the other residents buzzed with interest at dinner—they couldn't miss the striking resemblance I have to Clara, give or take a few wrinkles and my dark hair.*

Sitting at the desk, in the silence of the room, Sybil hears a tap on the door, soft at first and then more demanding. A wiry little lady stands in the hall offering a handshake when Sybil opens the door.

"My name is Biddy, short for Bridgett. I'm your next-door neighbour."

Sybil smiles and shakes Biddy's hand. "And I'm Clara's niece. What can I do for you?"

"I've come to tell you about Clara. We were friends, she and I. Something troubled her lately, I could tell. On dark evenings she walked in the cemetery. I can see it by lamplight from my window next door. She always walked straight down the main path, turned right at the tomb with the spire and went forward a couple of markers. After each visit, she came home and talked aloud as if she had someone visiting her."

"Maybe she did have a visitor. How would you know?"

"My dear…may I call you Sybil? I know because I can see the main staircase when my door is open just a little."

Sybil decides the lady from next door must be a snoop—harmless, likely, but still a busybody. She asks, "How did you know my name?"

"The grapevine, dearie, or perhaps Clara spoke of you. 'My favourite niece,' she used to say. You really do look like her. Here, I'm interrupting you. I must go. Still, I thought you should know that Clara could very well have had a ghost in here with her, so don't be surprised if something strange happens in the night. I sometimes hear noises through the wall. Lock your door. If she had listened to me, she wouldn't have been out there on the staircase in the dark giggling with that voice just before she stumbled."

"Clara had a visitor when she fell? The police report didn't mention anyone," says Sybil.

"But they know. I told them about the ghosts," says Biddy with impatience as she slips into her room.

Sybil locks the door and returns to sorting papers from Clara's desk. She divides them into two boxes, saving those things of value and discarding the rest. Perched on the corner of the desk, a picture of herself and Clara in Atlanta distracts her. The black hair falling in soft waves, the slender face and captivating eyes, the fine line of the eyebrows, nose and mouth…these descriptions, she feels, are Clara's. To see herself in mirror image seems vain. When she plucks up the picture to drop it into a box, a second photo, an old black-and-white portrait, falls from inside the cardboard folder. On the back of the picture Clara has inscribed,

Dear Sybil, meet your great-grandmother, Annette. We three ladies look alike, the Devereaux image through

*and through. Perhaps you will meet her and my friends
in the park across the street. I hope so.
Love, Clara*

*The cemetery? She calls the cemetery a park with "friends"?
Clara once mentioned that Great Grandma Annette died of a
broken heart seventy years ago when her husband never came
home from the Great War. Clara hopes I'll meet Annette? Poor
Clara! When she wrote this note she must have been hallucinating about Annette and friends in the park, just like Biddy.* Sybil
returns to sorting papers.

The door lock clicks. Sybil jumps. A man enters.

"I'm so sorry, ma'am. I didn't think you were coming
until tomorrow. I'm Gerard, the handyman. Mrs. Lord lets
me live in a little room under the staircase. I loaned Clara a
hammer, and I want it back."

"You have a key to Clara's room?" Sybil shoots back.

"Yes. The landlady and I both have keys. You never know
when the plumbing might burst or the roof leak. Things go
wrong in these old houses."

Sybil notices that the man, maybe fifty, seems nervous.
He keeps flicking his eyes toward Clara's hope chest.

"I haven't seen a hammer. Did she say why she wanted
one? That might give us a clue where to look for it."

They search the closet and various drawers but find no
hammer. Sybil thinks it odd when Gerard stumbles against
the corner of the hope chest that he could have passed by with
ease. When they fail to find the hammer, he insists that he'll
be back in the morning to finish the search.

As soon as Gerard leaves, Sybil goes to the hand-carved
chest and tries the lid. It opens easily to reveal Clara's treasures. Poor soul—a shabby patchwork quilt, yellowed linens

embroidered with "D" for Devereaux, a book of poetry, and frilly underthings of a bygone era. It truly had been her hope chest, never fulfilled.

Sybil begins to repack the items she'd removed. The smell of cedar floats on the air. When her hand stretches deep to the bottom of the chest but not to floor level, she wonders if it has a false bottom. She examines the interior and searches for a hidden release in the exquisite pattern carved into the top and sides of the chest. The bottom moulding does not align at one end. She tugs, and a drawer slides open. Had Gerard stumbled against the chest in a vain effort to hide the drawer by kicking it shut? Possibly, she thinks.

Green felt lines the drawer. At one end Sybil finds a broken string of pearls, an ivory-backed mirror and comb showing the family monogram of "D," a set of tarnished lady's silver cuff links, three flamboyant hat pins and a cracked cameo with a broken clasp. She looks at the useless heirlooms and wonders if Clara, with all her beauty, had ever known happy times and gifts from caring suitors. It seems unlikely from the items displayed before her.

Ten thirty—time for bed. I'll start again tomorrow when I'm fresh, she decides with a sigh. *Funny, if Clara fell at night and the police closed the room immediately, who made the bed? Perhaps, if something was worrying Clara, as Biddy says, she might not have opened the bed before she fell. Then again, with Mrs. Lord and Gerard both having keys…*Sybil squeezes her forehead between both hands. *Questions, questions, so many questions…they'll just have to wait.* She throws the bedcovers back, climbs in and plumps the pillow under her head.

Her hand hits something hard under the pillow. The hammer! Clara hid the hammer under the pillow? But why? To ward off an attacker? Sybil crosses to the door and checks the lock a second time. She turns out the light and forces her eyes shut with the hope of going to sleep.

A constantly rattling shutter wakes Sybil at dawn. Thin grey light holds the room in suspension until she realizes her whereabouts. Thoughts of yesterday crowd into her sleepy brain. How could she have slept so soundly? Biddy's ghosts must have stayed home or else weren't up to the job of causing a disturbance loud enough to trouble her sound sleep. Such nonsense. She laughs to herself with the thought of ghosts banging the shutter.

The chime on the downstairs clock summons the residents to breakfast. They stare when Sybil arrives with a hammer. No one speaks to her until after breakfast when an elderly gentleman joins her on the staircase.

"My name is Raymond. I live below in the formal parlour. Clara and I were very close friends. I wonder if I could have a word with you in private."

Raymond continues up the stairs with Sybil and drops his last remark just as Sybil unlocks the door to Clara's room. She feels obliged to ask him in. Despite his growing years, Raymond looks like a lumberjack, with strong shoulders, big hands and a lean body. His piercing blue eyes melt with softness as he declares his love for Clara.

"Our friendship started the day she moved in, ten years ago. We read to each other and visited on the front porch. She liked me but wouldn't let me court her. She said old ladies needed contentment, not sex. I hope you don't find the word 'sex' offensive, Miss Sybil. Clara wouldn't even let me hold her hand when we went walking in the park. That's what we call the cemetery, the park. It's a nice place to visit—very peaceful for a walk. We would read the names and inscriptions and visit our own family tombs quite often. You might say I'm just waiting to cross the street for home. Clara waited the same as I. Now she's gone, and I'll never know her shapely body."

The man gives Sybil the creeps—one moment talking of sex, the next of death. With so much power in his body, she can see why Clara might want the hammer.

Sybil cuts him short. "Is this why you wished to speak to me, or have you another reason for coming up here?"

"Please, don't think me silly, but could I have her nightie? Now that she's gone, I could caress it and fantasize a little. What harm would it do to humour an old man? I think I'd like the pink nightie. I've seen it through the window from the garden. It should be in that drawer over there."

My god, thinks Sybil, *all the residents know this room. He likely came on to Clara and scared her to death. The hammer must have been to ward him off if he ever tried to bed her.*

Without another word, Raymond crosses to the bureau, opens a drawer and takes a nightie in his hands. Sybil steps up to stop him, but his massive frame towers over hers. He sidesteps and disappears out the door.

"They're all crazy here," Sybil mumbles, and she locks the door as if to put a barrier between her and the other residents. No sooner has the door lock clicked than someone starts to knock.

"It's me, Gerard, the handyman. I said I'd be back this morning." Sybil lets him in. "Thanks for the hammer," he continues as the door opens. "Where did you find it?"

Sybil dislikes the question. She hardly wants to say "under the pillow," so she says, "On the floor at the foot of the bed near the hope chest."

Gerard continues to stand there as if he expects more from his visit to Clara's room. He looks uncomfortable. Why doesn't he leave?

"Did she have anything more of yours?" Sybil asks, her annoyance hardly masked.

"No. No, I just thought," the man stammers, "that maybe I could help you with moving boxes or something."

Truly annoyed with the man's persistence in hanging around, Sybil moves towards the door. She feels sure that Gerard has snooped through the room on other occasions and wants a chance to claim more loot. His tell-tale eyes prove that he knows about the secret drawer in the hope chest. *Perhaps that's why there's nothing of value left in the drawer,* she considers. *He's been spiriting things away bit by bit. Perhaps Clara caught him in the act, and he did her in to save his job.*

"No, Gerard, I can manage. Once the moving company comes for the furniture, there won't be much left. Thanks anyway," and she shows him the door.

Sybil fusses with her thoughts…Biddy, with her tale of voices on the stairs and her ghost theory; Raymond and Gerard—they all had reason to trouble Clara. Perhaps one of them pushed her down the stairs to hide a secret. *I must go to the police and tell them I suspect foul play,* she decides.

❦

At ten o'clock, the officer on duty at the downtown police station ushers Sybil into Detective Hallett's office. She discloses her doubts about Clara's "accidental" fall.

"Miss Devereaux, Biddy tells everyone about ghosts. She's great for the tourist trade but hardly believable. As for the other two gentlemen, Raymond and Gerard, they have clean records. We have no reason to suspect them when there is no evidence against them and only your word against theirs in the possibility of foul play. No, I'm sorry, painful as it may be to accept, I'm sure your aunt simply stumbled on the stairs for reasons unknown—sleepwalking, perhaps. Thank you for bringing these matters to my attention, but as you can see, we've already done a thorough job of investigating the matter. The case is closed." With his final words, the detective moves to the door and opens it to signal that the interview is over.

Defeated by the macho authority of the detective's voice, Sybil asks the cab driver to take her directly back to the antebellum house. The taxi stops directly in front of the main entrance to the cemetery. In large print a sign proclaims "City of the Dead" to excite the tourist trade. For some reason Sybil feels ready to enter the cemetery. She thinks of Biddy's words and decides to take the same route. "Down the main path to the tomb with the spire," she recites. "Turn right and pass two tombs."

There, to her surprise, Sybil finds a modest-sized tomb inscribed with the name "Devereaux." The tomb shines white in the sun, with an elegant family crest carved on the panel of the central door. Sybil reads the names of her forefathers, including Annette's. Then it strikes her! City officials, or the lawyer who handled Clara's burial until they located her, the executor, must have interred her aunt in the tomb. Clara's remains are here, right in front of her, inside the tomb, still fresh on the grate, like the cab driver suggested, "rotting in the summer sun." Sybil, convulsed with the thought, rushes from the cemetery.

In the lower hall she comes upon Mrs. Lord, elegantly dressed as if going to a special function. Their eyes meet with a cordial good morning. Then Sybil notices the exquisite gold timepiece pinned to the landlady's bosom. She knows she saw the locket-style watch on Clara's dress years before in Atlanta.

"Why Mrs. Lord, your timepiece has the Devereaux family crest on it. Clara had a piece just like that."

Mrs. Lord assumes a defensive attitude.

"You're quite right, my dear, but she gave it to me," and with that she storms out and slams the door.

"Gave it to you," Sybil mutters to the empty foyer. "That's the last thing Clara would give away. Ten years ago she said she wanted me to have it."

Sybil's thoughts race ahead of her as she runs up the stairs. *Has Mrs. Lord been snooping in the room too? They're all hiding something. Some justice! The police won't help. They'll say "her word against mine."*

With a vengeance, Sybil sorts, saves or discards the last few items in Clara's room—the sooner she leaves the old house, the better. She contacts the cemetery service and arranges for Clara's name to be engraved on the tomb. She asks the movers to come the following day, and she lines up a second-hand furniture dealer to take the pieces on consignment.

❦

Meals continue in frigid silence. Gerard, Raymond and Biddy all act as if they sense her distrust of them and refuse to look her way. More and more, Sybil feels sure that Clara's death has been no accident and that the police prefer a closed case to a proper investigation. They are likely thinking that nothing would be gained by searching for a suspect among any of these old souls. Sybil can see that she's come up against a wall of hometown silence. The police and residents want only to see her finish clearing the room and go on her way.

After the furniture van leaves late the next day, Sybil orders a cab to arrive at seven thirty p.m. As the last rays of sun begin to form long shadows, she crosses the street, wheeling her suitcase, and returns to Clara's tomb. With tears in her eyes and hands clasped at her bosom, she speaks aloud in the direction of the tomb.

"Goodbye, sweet Clara. I'm sorry I couldn't unmask your murderer. Please don't feel I let you down."

"Don't cry, my dear," comes a voice that surrounds her. Sybil wheels around and sees no one at first.

"Over here, Sybil. I hoped you would come for this visit. Please meet your great-grandmother, Annette."

Sybil tries not to believe her ears. Then she sees two ladies, mirror images of each other, in the shadow of the tomb, ethereal in quality.

Sybil feels her forehead. *Is the heat getting to me? Am I talking to a ghost?*

"Don't worry, Sybil. It is I, Clara, and Annette."

That voice again. *Surely I'm hallucinating, but it sounds so clear.*

Not sure what's happening, through tears, Sybil again apologizes to Clara for not finding the guilty one who pushed her down the stairs.

"Did Biddy not tell you? Annette and I were having a visit in my room and I decided to walk her home. I stumbled on the top step, plain and simple."

"How awful!"

"Not at all, my dear. I've been looking forward to such an event. We're happy here in the park."

"Annette," asks Sybil, "why didn't Biddy tell me she saw you? She spoke only of voices."

"Poor dear, you don't understand," says Annette. "Biddy's not one of us, not like you, Clara and me. She senses us, but she can't see us like you can. You're special, just as we hoped you would be."

Sybil swings between confusion and amazement. To prolong the moment while she sorts her thoughts she asks Clara questions. "What about the hammer? You must have expected Raymond to sneak into your room at night. Why, that depraved man wanted one of your nighties to caress!"

"Dear Raymond. Yes, that sounds like Raymond. You mustn't worry about him. It's just that a man's hormones are active so much later in life than a woman's. With his virility, I couldn't give him an inch. If ever he had me in bed he would have crushed me to death. Why, the very size of him made him a risk. I'm sure he's delighted to have my nightie to keep his testosterone buzzing."

Certainly, in bygone years Clara was no prude, thinks Sybil, but to hear her as a ghost, still rattling on as if she were part of this world, confuses Sybil even more.

"And that Gerard!" says Sybil. "He tried to sneak into your room when he thought I hadn't arrived. He certainly knew his way around. I know he knew about the secret drawer in your hope chest, because he tried to kick it shut. Why, there's nothing left of value in it. I suspect he stole all of your special pieces."

"No, my dear. Gerard knew his way about my room because I asked him to fix things for me. Just last week he mended the drawer in the hope chest so you would be able to sell it. That's when I stole his hammer. Yet, the dear boy told you he loaned it to me. How sweet of him. He lied to protect my thievery. Over the years, board and room expenses took more and more of my old age pension, so I pawned pieces of jewellery when I needed extra money. Now, with nothing left, making ends meet has been quite a trouble to me these last few months, until the accident on the stairs released me to be here with Annette."

"What about Mrs. Lord? She's wearing your favourite brooch—that lovely gold timepiece with the Devereaux crest. She said you gave it to her."

"And so I did. She accepted the watch in lieu of last month's rent. I so wanted a new dress for my burial that I spent my pension on this lovely gown and had nothing else to offer for room and board."

"If there's nothing left in your estate, why did you have me as executor? The city managed your burial very well. They could have cleared your room, too."

"Don't you see, dear Sybil? Your identical likeness to Annette and me makes you the third 'special' lady in the Devereaux family. We knew as executor you'd likely come to New Orleans. We wanted an opportunity to have this visit with you, but you had to make it happen, which you did by coming after sundown. You can understand why we seldom go visiting by daylight. You must promise to join us when you leave your earthly realm so we three may watch the passage of time together. We'll be waiting for you. You'll like it here, Sybil. Goodbye for now."

With that the two ladies fade into the wall of the tomb. Sybil wipes her eyes to clear her vision and looks around. Fingers of dusk have settled over the cemetery. She sees no one near the tomb. The tombstones in darkness give her the shivers, yet she senses a strange comfort from them.

Sybil mutters, "This is nonsense; one does not talk to ghosts," yet she feels confused.

Alone, she tugs on her suitcase and walks through the shadows of the cemetery toward the gate. She hears soft murmuring to her left and looks across the cemetery. A few tombs over, a couple walk hand in hand. The woman wears a hoop skirt and carries a parasol even though the sun has set. They nod cordially to her.

"Good evening, Miss Sybil," floats on the soft breeze.

With her outfit and his black suit and ruffled shirt, they could have been straight off the movie set of *Gone with the Wind*. When Sybil stares at them, they disappear as if demolecularized in *Star Trek*'s transporter.

A five-year-old, clutching the hand of his baby sister, tugs on Sybil's sleeve. Both children wear white dresses tied with a wide white sash in the style for children's burials in the nineteenth century.

"I'm Tom, and this is Cassie," says the boy. "Are you our mother? We died of cholera in 1873, when we came to the new country. We've been waiting for Mother a long time, but we don't know what she'll look like, so we ask everyone we see."

Sybil feels a second, more urgent, tug on her sleeve. "Please, ma'am, are you our mother?"

Before Sybil can answer, the children vanish.

Sybil squeezes her eyes shut. *Did the child's voice come from an apparition? I'm sure I heard it. Did I really see them? I know I felt the boy tug on my sleeve.*

Not sure if she lives with substance or walks as a ghost, Sybil realizes that the couple in the park were Clara's "friends." *That couple knew me. They used my name. If Clara told them about me, why did they disappear?* Her jumbled thoughts become so foreign to her former way of thinking that they numb her brain. *Am I already a ghost?*

Her cab waits at the curb. Sybil climbs in and wonders if the cabby will see her as mortal. He turns his head and looks into the back seat.

"Where to, ma'am?" he asks with a smile.

II

BREAK AND ENTER

Ashley sleeps uneasily. She rises to go to the bathroom. Her white T-shirt nightie can be seen through her window. Her pink curtains don't close, but who cares? No one looks in a second-storey window at 2 a.m.

Outside in lofty trees, wind moans softly through the backyards of old narrow houses built shoulder to shoulder, their peeling white paint and state of disrepair highlighted among the shadows by the light of the half- moon that shines on the low-rent residences for university students.

The motion light in the backyard flashes. Ashley glances towards the window. *Probably a cat.* She decides that going to the bathroom is more important.

On her return, the light flashes again. At first, she sits on the edge of her bed, wondering which of her boyfriends will invited her to the fall prom. Then she decides to take another look through the window towards the garage at the end of the yard, which the landlord did not include in the rental agreement.

Her view includes high solid board fences running down each side of the narrow lot, enclosing a tangle of grass and weeds. A light breeze flutters the leaves, changing them from black to silver in the white moonlight. *Nothing out there,* she thinks, but the motion light flashes again. Uneasy, Ashley slips quietly to her housemate's neighbouring bedroom.

"Janet. Wake up! The motion light in the backyard has been flashing."

Janet pushes back her calico comforter but does not bother to open her eyes. "Forget it; I have a test in the morning. It's likely wind in the leaves." She flips her shiny black hair and turns over, feigning sleep.

"I bet it goes again, Janet. Maybe it's me at the window setting it off. You take a look."

Janet peeks through the corner of her window. When Ashley stands at the window in her bedroom, the light flashes. Ashley sprints into the darkness of her friend's bedroom.

"Something strange is going on, Janet. I don't like it. We should never have asked Henry to install that motion light and the security system on the doors. Ever since then, he's been different. He barks at us. Landlords don't have a special right to be miserable."

"That's just Henry, Ashley—military-like. He inherited this dump when his mother died and hates spending a dime on it. I guess we just pushed his buttons the wrong way by asking for protection. Go to bed."

Ashley can't sleep. The hairs on the back of her neck prickle. In the darkness of the silent house, she feels sure that her ears would hear one drip from the kitchen faucet.

Then it comes—a distant click—the click of the bolt action in a lock.

Did I really hear a click? Thoughts swirl through Ashley's head as she strains to listen. *It can't be the front or back door; the security system is turned on. It must be that cursed door that*

Henry built into the basement this fall and laughed it off, saying "Not to worry. How else can I make repairs now that you have that security *system?" What could we say? The steps outside down to the doorway into the basement appeared the day after we signed the lease and asked for the system.*

Ashley tries to calm herself. She knows that the bottom hinge of "Henry's" door squeaks. *Surely, I'll hear it if someone opens the door.* Her mind keeps bouncing like a ping-pong ball. *Only Henry has a key. Would he come at 2 a.m.? He's so strong, and Janet and I are so petite—maybe he's trying to scare us so we'll move. Then he could rent to someone else, up the price, say that we were the ones who broke the lease, and keep our security payment.*

"Oh stop it," she scolds aloud, "you're getting all wound up. You'll hear the hinge if someone's there." She calms down, but still she listens.

Was that a squeak?

Heart pounding, Ashley races to Janet's room.

"Shhh, Janet. I think someone is in the house. I heard Henry's door hinge squeak." They listen but hear nothing.

The girls creep to the top of the stairs to listen. The cold October air coming through Ashley's window freezes their butts, but still they stand there with bare feet, statues in the dark, listening, peering down into the black depths of the stairwell.

In the basement, footsteps scrape on the concrete floor. Ashley gasps. Without saying a word, Janet takes her cellphone into the bathroom, closes the door and calls 9-1-1. The girls slip into shoes and sweatsuits and hide in Janet's closet.

"If someone wants to sneak into the basement," whispers Ashley, "why would they scrape their feet? There's nothing down there to interest them, just four concrete walls, a washer, dryer, gas water heater and furnace—nothing!"

They feel vulnerable, trapped on the second floor at the top of a narrow staircase if the intruder comes after them. They open the closet door a crack to listen for the intruder's approach. They know that the third step on the staircase creaks.

Again, they hear footsteps on concrete, then the rub of wood on wood.

"What's that noise?" Ashley whispers to Janet.

"I think someone opened the small window on the basement wall," comes a soft reply. They open the closet door a crack wider to listen.

"What's taking the police so long?" murmurs Janet.

The doorbell rings.

"The police! Ashley, how do you answer a doorbell if you think there's a rapist in your house?"

Ashley listens—hears nothing—hopes the doorbell has frightened the intruder away. In the dark, she tiptoes down the stairs to answer the doorbell.

She sees two policemen through the spyhole. Ashley disengages the security system so it won't scream and opens the door. The policemen seem very young. One blushes at seeing blonde Ashley, who's about his own age.

The policemen enter the dark hall. The senior officer flips the light switch beside the door to reveal the tired green paint and brown stained staircase.

"Someone came into our basement through the landlord's private door," says Ashley.

Janet has joined them, and the foursome gathers in the basement. The officers find no intruder. A matchbook lies flipped open on the gas heater. The small window, set high on the wall, is open wide, and the door is locked.

"We didn't leave matches on the heater. We're not that stupid," says Janet. "And the window was closed and locked this afternoon when I was down here, and *now* it's open."

With a smile, the "blushing" officer hands the matches to Ashley and closes the window. The other officer speaks.

"That's an illegal entrance if you girls, as renters, don't have a key. We'll have to tell the landlord about that when we report your nine-eleven call." He takes out his notebook. After writing for a few minutes he asks for the landlord's name.

"It's Henry Dooprey," says Ashley.

The officer writing in his notebook blanches. The younger officer blurts out, "That's our staff sergeant!"

"He's a policeman?" squeals Janet. "We've never seen him in uniform. He wears jeans and says he does shift work."

The younger policeman seems about to speak when the other one coughs as if to say, "Shut your mouth." The senior officer doesn't ask any more questions about Henry.

"One other person has a key as well," says Janet. "Her name is Ruby Spragg. She dyes her hair ruby red. "

The younger officer explodes again. "That's our sergeant!" The officer taking notes lifts his eyes to heaven as if asking God for relief from his partner's naive outbursts.

In the silence, Janet continues. "Ruby's supposed to do odd jobs around the place. She never does anything, yet she's here all the time."

Annoyed by Ruby's duplicity, Ashley takes over from Janet. "She says she does gigs at city nightclubs. I bet she hangs around until we leave, then phones Henry for a little go on the sofa—and Henry's married at that—a wife and three kids!"

Janet joins in facetiously. "No, no, Ashley. They come in here to practice lap dancing."

"Now, ladies, that's just your imagination talking," says the older officer. "The only thing I can report for sure is what you say about the motion light and the sound of a key in the door, which is now locked. We see that a window is open, and we found matches on the heater, both of which you say are new developments. Even if someone came in, they might have crawled in the window. We haven't found much hard evidence. If it's all right with you, I'd like to talk it over with Staff Sergeant Dooprey before we make our report."

Ashley can see that the policeman is manipulating the evidence to mean nothing—their word against Henry's—yet she's sure that Henry's behind the disturbance. He could have been controlling the motion light from the garage. She is still convinced that Henry is trying to frighten them so they'll move. She knows they should disagree with the officer about talking the case over with Henry, but confronted with the dominance that a police uniform presents, they agree to the officer's request. He hands Ashley his card, and the policemen leave.

Too wound up to sleep, the girls sit at the kitchen table with milk and toasted raisin bread. As if struck with the same thought, they grab a kitchen chair and return to the basement. What if Henry is angry and returns? He'll know about the 9–1–1 call from listening to the police radio band. With all their strength, they wedge the chair under the doorknob of Henry's illegal door and return to the kitchen.

"Agreeing with that cop isn't right, Janet. To save their own skins, those policemen won't confront Henry. Their report will be conveniently lost in paperwork."

Janet dials the number on the card the policeman left and tells his answering machine that they have changed their minds—that they want the 9–1–1 call reported just like it would be for anyone else.

"So much for phoning the police," says Ashley. "They can still hush the whole thing. If we can't trust them to deal with Henry, who can we trust?"

The disgruntled girls sit eyeing the chipped green kitchen cupboards, the faded yellow tulips on the wallpaper and the old grey linoleum.

Bang, bang, bang! Someone is trying to kick down the basement door. In a panic, Janet jumps to turn off the lights.

"That chair under the knob will keep him busy," she whispers. "We've gotta get out of here!"

They run to the front hall closet. Janet grabs a jacket and turns toward the door to disengage the alarm system so the intruder won't know they are escaping.

"That chair isn't going to hold the door forever, Ashley." *Bang—bang, bang!* "What's keeping you?"

"OK, OK, I'm coming," Ashley whispers. "As long as he's still kicking and pounding the door, I figured I had time to find the jacket that has my wallet and the remote control for relocking the door." They slip out of the front door, close it quietly, jump down the front steps and head for the neighbour's low picket fence. Once over the fence, they push themselves into the far side of a lilac bush to catch their breath and hide while they determine their next move.

"Push the remote, Ashley! Lock the front door. I'm sure I heard him burst through just as we left. With the door locked, he'll search the house for us. That will give us more time to get away."

The lights in the front hall landing flash on.

Janet grabs Ashley's arm. "Come on. We have to keep moving." Tucked into the shadow of the house, they run across the neighbour's lawn and sidle up directly behind a huge elm tree on the boulevard. Janet flits on to hide behind the next tree.

As lights continue to go on in the house, the girls work their way down the street like soldiers in a do-or-die war movie, in unison, crouched and darting to hide behind one tree after another. A block away, after peeking through the shop window to see that Henry isn't inside, they enter the bright lights of a twenty-four-hour convenience store. There are no customers. The clerk is half-asleep. He ignores them as they move to the back of the shop.

Ashley plugs money into the coffee machine. Exhausted, they sit on the ledge at the bottom of the magazine rack, out of sight, to sip their coffee while they collect their thoughts.

Ashley sighs. "We lost, and Henry won, Janet. We'll have to move now. I don't trust that house or Henry any more. Let's call a cab and get out of here before Henry comes looking for us."

After a short silence, Janet pounds a fist into the air. "No, we haven't lost! Tomorrow I'll phone Legal Aid and dump it all in some lawyer's lap. He'll take it to a prosecutor. I saw the name of the construction truck leaving the day that door was installed. The work order signed by Henry should be one day later than our lease agreement, and when they investigate, the illegal door should look damaged. That should prove something. We'll teach Staff Sergeant Henry Dooprey what 'break and enter' means!"

III

VISUAL JUDGEMENTS

I like the phone to ring, because it brings a visit with no visual impact. Callers can't see my tired eyes or my thinning brown hair above a face round with steroids; nor can I read the thoughts their eyes might reveal. There's the phone now.

The caller is a ski buddy. My old skiing group wants me to have lunch with them. I haven't seen them since the last time we skied together a year ago when my feet first gave me trouble. The doctor diagnosed the problem as an autoimmune disease. My immune system is attacking the nerves in my feet—neuropathy, like a paralysis. The specialists say my condition is unique because it doesn't respond to the usual treatments. They don't know how to contain the further nerve damage that is likely to occur in my hands next. All they can do is keep me on steroids. Somehow my appearance and condition embarrass me because I used to be so healthy. Should I reveal myself to them and agree to lunch? I have spent the year trying to learn how to cope with the new paralyzed me. This will be my first outing except with family.

She offers to come for me. "I still drive," I respond, inwardly proud of this one little victory.

Undeterred, she insists on picking me up at noon. Why can't others recognize that people with physical handicaps are forever setting little goals of independence for themselves so that they can attain little victories?

∽∞∾

At the restaurant, lights play on hanging green plants. Pictures adorn the polished oak panelling. Soft music plays as I enter awkwardly with my braces and crutches. The other three women are already seated. I feel sure that the noon crowd hushes with curiosity as my friends rise to welcome me. I see compassion in their eyes and want to say, "Don't pamper me or show concern; it cracks the veneer I have built around my world. Pretend I'm the old me."

I can see questions in their eyes. I know they know about my illness, but perhaps they have never really understood its far-reaching effects. Again, I want to say, "My health problem is complex and unending. If answers to your questions grow too long, push my 'off' button by showing interest in the conversation at the other end of the table. I will recognize that you have reached your limit of listening. I know that people like me, who live in relative isolation, often talk too long."

With difficulty, I make my way between the tables. As I arrive there is a pause when no one says anything. It's not the first time this has happened. I know they are astonished to see how much I have failed. They simply don't know what to say. In my head, I tell them, "My mundane world has a vibrant garden of memories budding hope for the future. I know you are busy with your day-to-day lives. Don't concern yourself about not calling these past many months, for every day, I visit with you in my garden."

I lay my crutches aside. One of them pulls the chair out for me. As I seat myself, holding fast to the edge of the table, their eyes follow in case I should stumble. I nearly scream, "Don't pamper me or show concern…it cracks my veneer," but I steady my voice and say what's in my heart. "How wonderful to see you all."

Again, there is that unmistakable pause when they are unsure of what to say next. I help them out. "How are your families? What's the snow on the hills like this year? Oh, we have so many things to talk about. What a great idea to get together."

With this cue, conversations begin. Again, I am the old me having lunch with my friends, even though my crutches are waiting for me under the table.

IV

THE ACCOMPLISHED MAFIA MOLL

For the first time in her life Marjorie Maynard felt like a businesswoman, as she started the sixty-minute commute from her country subdivision to the city of Houston. She wore the most professional outfit she could find in her wardrobe. The mint-green suit topped by a black gabardine coat complemented her greying hair, which she coiffed artistically to flatter her regal features. It was just six weeks ago, she remembered, when she announced to her husband that she needed a new goal in life.

"Property management, Calvin. I'm going to become a property manager. Now that the children have grown up, I need something challenging to fill my day."

Lowering his stock report, Calvin replied, with the wink of an eye, "You've always been a stay-at-home mother, and a good one, too, just like your mother before you. So how do you propose to make the transition from homemaker and charity worker to businesswoman, my dear?"

"Don't tease, Calvin. I'm serious. At my age there has to be more to life than keeping a spotless home. I thought

I could start by renting our condo in town now that we've moved out here."

"Madam Landlady, is it? If that's what you've decided, it's fine with me, and good luck to you. It's not an easy business. Some renters view life differently than we do. You'll find that life today is a lot different than the old days back in Canada."

⌒∞⌒

Madam Landlady, indeed! Marjorie laughed to herself as she moved along with the traffic on the freeway. Never mind. Calvin would soon change with the times and learn to use the words "property manager."

Sparse traffic allowed her thoughts to focus on her business situation. No one could say she'd never done anything in her life. She'd served her husband and family well, the community too. For years she'd planned the museum's auction and organized the city's residential drive for cancer, as well as working for Big Sisters. But those were all volunteer jobs—jobs where, regardless of competency, you received compliments. She never felt tested or fulfilled. She needed to know she was equal to the modern perception of a capable woman. Perhaps in her own business, with her own money at stake, she would feel she'd achieved something.

With Calvin's recent transfer, Marjorie's old friends and volunteer activities were a thousand miles away from Texas. During the months of temporary living in the condo, she hadn't minded the change. Organizing the décor of their new home and working with the builders filled her day. Now that they were settled in the house, she felt the urge to do something to satisfy her own needs.

The traffic lights changed. *Won't Calvin be surprised when he phones from Toronto and hears I've collected next month's rent!*

Marjorie arranged everything at the condo—the redecorating, the furnishings—interviewed the tenants who answered her ad, signed the lease with the nicest fellow, Robert Barker, and promised to come by today and see if everything was satisfactory. Her thoughts shifted to her new tenant and his family and what she knew about them.

Yes, Mr. Barker said he came from Orlando and that he served as lay preacher in a church near the condo. "Church Of The Resurrection," she thought he called it. His wife, in her plain blue dress, hardly spoke but appeared pleased with the arrangements. Their little girl seemed shy. The poor little thing looked undernourished.

Marjorie parked her yellow sports car in front of the third unit in a neat row of townhouses. She rang the bell. The door opened a crack to reveal Mrs. Barker pushing back her hair and fussing with the collar of her wrinkled blouse as she peered through the narrow opening.

"Oh, it's you, Mrs. Maynard," she said in a loud voice, her head turned so the name carried into the condo. "Is it the first of the month already?"

Marjorie could hear scurrying in the other rooms as the door slowly opened, exposing the unkempt woman. *Perhaps they've been caught by surprise,* Marjorie thought, and she took extra time in removing her coat. Newspapers cluttered the hall table. She could see dirty dishes on the counter in the kitchen. A beer bottle lay on its side at the end of the couch. Drab little Ellie slipped away to the kitchen after some hidden command from her mother. In the silence, Marjorie thought she heard the buzz of an electric shaver.

Mr. Barker emerged from the back of the condo, lowering his hands from the final button of his shirt.

"How nice to see you, Mrs. Maynard," he said in his cordial preacher's voice. "Kate, get the lady some coffee."

He talked constantly—Sorry the condo looked a little messy...working very hard at church...getting Ellie into school...Kate looking for work.

Marjorie remembered that Kate claimed to be a church worker too but let the remark pass. Perhaps she misunderstood them the day of the interview.

As the coffee arrived, the doorbell rang. Kate returned from the front hall, her eyes wide with fear.

"Bert, the man at the door wants you. Something tells me it's *him*. I asked him to wait until the landlady left. What'll we do?"

Mr. Barker turned to Marjorie. "We have someone at the door from the church. He insists on coming in, and as the pastor I can't turn him away. He's a man who gets very angry, sometimes violent. I wish he hadn't come here at all, but he has. Would you do us the favour of keeping Ellie for an hour or so? She's only seven, and we don't like her exposed to this type of person. Perhaps it would be best if you pick her up at the back door in case he makes a scene. We have your address. I'll come for her in a little while and finish our business then."

What can I say? thought Marjorie. *Ellie is such a quiet little thing, and Kate's fear is genuine.*

On her way out, Marjorie saw a bull-necked man standing beside a black van waiting at the curb. As she started her car and turned at the end of the block, she caught a glimpse of the man charging towards the house. Ellie and her mother waited outside at the back of the condo. Kate pushed Ellie into the sports car with admonitions to behave and rushed back into their unit.

On the highway, nearly home, Marjorie heard a heavy motor approaching quickly from behind. Glancing in her mirror, she saw a van pulling in behind her. It was the same black van she'd seen at the condo. Despite its speedy approach it did not pass.

She went faster. It went faster. She changed lanes. The van changed lanes. She slowed. It stayed behind her. *Why would he do that?* she wondered. *He has no business with me. With Ellie? It seemed unlikely.*

The van came so close that Marjorie could see the man's face in her mirror. His dark, beady eyes searched the interior of her car. He looked mean. *What if he approaches my car on foot during the next red light?* She felt nervous without cause, she told herself, yet the van continued to tail them. *Perhaps I should try to lose him like they do on TV,* she considered, laughing at her absurd solution. *But what else can I do? He scares me.*

Down the road at the next intersection, the traffic light had been green for a long time. It would change soon. Marjorie tramped on the accelerator and swung her car into the adjoining lane, passed two cars, and sped through the crossing on the stale amber light. The black van grew smaller in her rear-view mirror, trapped by the red light and traffic.

Up ahead, Marjorie could see the road sign marking their exit. She increased her speed to catch the green light and wheeled through the turn into a subdivision of expensive houses. One main road, some side streets, and she would be home.

All the while, Ellie said nothing, apparently unconcerned with the wild driving, as if that's how cars were meant to be driven. *Her father must be a terrible driver,* swept through Marjorie's hyperactive brain.

She checked her mirror again. Impossible—the black van was gaining on her, pursuing her. It made her feel hunted. She couldn't drive to the police station; her subdivision didn't have one. For that matter, there was nothing in their subdivision except expensive homes—no shopping mall, no gas station, nothing where she would find a helping hand.

Perhaps I can take a less direct route home and lose him again. With the zip of this sports car and our maze of streets, I might be able to manage it. That private school, I'll try it first, she said to herself, remembering the thick landscaping along its circular driveway.

Marjorie found herself gunning the agile sports model like a gangster in the get-away car of a bad movie. With abandon, she swung into the school's driveway and disappeared behind the wall of shrubs. The heavy van bolted past, brakes screaming. Marjorie completed the circle at top speed, barely keeping four wheels on the ground, and retraced her route back into the subdivision.

Her circuit through the school grounds gained a few seconds, but she felt sure he would catch up again. Adrenalin electrified her system. She had no experience in being pursued. To escape, she needed a plan to get home undetected.

A tall, dense hedge separated her driveway from the lane beside her home. *I'll go down that lane. As I pass the side of the garage, I'll push my electric door opener and start the door up, do a quick U-turn at the end of the lane into my driveway, and go right up into the garage. With the door closed, this yellow hot rod will vanish.*

She zigzagged through the neighbourhood, cutting the corners dangerously close. The van hung back, but she could see it creep around every corner in cunning pursuit. She hoped the short lane would give the seconds needed. She activated the garage door in passing, skidded the U-turn, and bounced to a halt, deep in the garage, with the door already descending.

Marjorie peeked out the garage window. She never knew her heart could pound so hard. The black van rumbled past in the lane. It stopped at the street corner, but it did not turn in. Hallelujah!

She led Ellie from the garage to the adjoining house, pulled the curtains in the family room at the back, and settled Ellie in front of the TV. Marjorie engaged the security system on the doors and windows, then peered carefully through the sheers that covered the picture window in the living room. The van was there. On her street—coasting past her house, checking driveways for the yellow car!

When the van reached the far end of the street, Marjorie pulled the velvet drapes behind the sheers. One by one, with the van out of sight, she closed all the drapes on the front of the house. She went to the garage and taped a black garbage bag over the window. If she could see out, then *he* might look in.

He? Who could he be? This is ridiculous—barricading my own house, and I don't even know why I'm hiding. I haven't done anything. How did I get into this predicament? she asked herself as she crept from window to window, taking a peek in each direction.

I suppose I should call the police, but what can I tell them? They will say it's my imagination, that I'm just nervous with Calvin out of town. Mr. Barker is the one I should phone. She dialled the condo. No answer. They must be on their way. She would just have to wait for him; after all, the house was secure.

Ellie sat quietly in the family room, subdued, really. She displayed no curiosity; nor did she ask questions. She seemed withdrawn, like some of the children at Big Sisters who came from troubled homes, yet Ellie's parents were stable. *I'm a stranger, and she's frightened,* Marjorie decided.

Suppertime came. Marjorie fixed some sandwiches and tried to be friendly as they sat closeted with the TV. Ellie had little to say. When the phone rang, she jumped and spilled her milk.

"Hello, Mrs. Maynard. Is Ellie behaving?"

"Thank goodness you've called, Mr. Barker. Please come for her. That dreadful man followed us from your place and is prowling our street. He doesn't know which house we're in, but what if he finds us? I'm sure he's still out there looking. I tried to phone you, but no one answered."

"That must have been when we left the condo to come, but our old clunker wouldn't start. I'll have to do some work on it. Do you think Ellie will be all right? It may take until morning."

"But what about the man in the black van?" her voice strained in reply. "I'm all alone here. My husband's away on business."

"I'll come tonight then, by ten o'clock, if I can."

Nothing more will go wrong, Marjorie convinced herself. *I've managed to fool the man till now, so I can likely fool him a few more hours.*

From the corner of her window, she could see the van parked down the street. *The TV will have to go off if I'm to have him think that no one is home. It's getting dark, and the light of the screen will show.* Ellie wouldn't mind. She had fallen asleep on the sofa. Marjorie covered the child with a blanket and considered the coming night. The man had not found them, and the alarm would warn the police if anyone tried to break in. She curled up on the other end of the sofa and watched the evening shadows grow as she waited for Ellie's father.

Bang, bang, bang, came a knock of authority at the door. Marjorie froze—11 p.m. She must have dozed. Mr. Barker wouldn't come that late. She peeked through the security viewer in the door. Without her porch light, she saw the faint outline of a heavyset man. Oh, please have him go away.

Bang! Bang! Bang!

Marjorie didn't move a muscle. She doubted she could have. Her chest ached. She had forgotten to breathe. Thank goodness the noise hadn't awakened Ellie.

The man turned and scuffed his way down the concrete steps. Five minutes later, Marjorie crept to her darkened second-floor bedroom and peeked out, lifting only the corner of the curtain. The van wasn't there. She had fooled him.

Her adrenalin settled a little. She carried the sleeping child up to the guest room and tucked her into bed. Ellie seemed so wan and unloved with stringy hair trailing across her sallow cheek.

Marjorie tiptoed into the master bedroom. She should try to get some sleep. What else could she do in a darkened house? Ellie would be fine until morning, she convinced herself.

Sleep did not come easily. Marjorie was just drifting off when the bedside phone electrified every nerve in her body. She dared not answer it if she wanted that man to think that no one was home. In a panic, she stuffed the phone under her pillow and prayed for the ringing to stop before it woke Ellie.

Thoughts ricocheted through her brain. What had she got herself into? Perhaps she should phone the police. The phone call might have been Calvin. He might worry. *Maybe I should call the police, but what would I tell them?* She tried to settle her thoughts. With the electronic security system to protect them, they should be fine. She mustn't let the darkness allow her imagination to get the upper hand. She would think more clearly in the morning. After all, the man had left, hadn't he? If anyone tried to break in, she told herself over and over, the alarm would save them. She forced her head to relax on the cool pillow. She must get some sleep.

Sleep never did come. At six forty-five she heard a motor at the front of the house. Cautiously, she slid the curtain aside. A dark-blue panel truck with rusted fenders waited in her driveway. It faced out to the road with the motor running, ready to be on its way.

The doorbell rang. The black van was nowhere in sight. Marjorie hurried into her dressing gown, peeked through the viewer to see Mr. Barker, and unlocked the door.

"Sorry I didn't make it last night. I hope coming this early isn't inconvenient. It's an hour's drive, and I must be at work by eight. Is Ellie awake?"

The child appeared, unwashed and lethargic. With breakfast declined, the two started to leave.

"What about the rent?" Marjorie asked.

"Don't worry; it will be in the mail this morning," he said, patting her on the arm in assurance as he herded the sleepy child through the doorway.

Marjorie sighed with relief and returned to her bed. At least she had managed, and it was over. Calvin would be proud of her.

At eight o'clock, the door chimes startled her. Again she checked for the black van, then opened the door. A young policeman eyed her closely.

"Good morning, Mrs. Maynard. Our records show you own a yellow Cobra GT. I have a search warrant here. Please excuse me; I must attend to it," and he darted up the stairs, two at a time.

The house isn't neat, the beds aren't made, Marjorie thought to herself, committed to having an immaculate home. *What on earth is he searching for?*

The policeman checked the garage for her car and then found the two milk glasses in the sink from last night's supper.

"Well, Mrs. Maynard, it would seem that two of you were here last night and you deliberately concealed your car. We're acting on a kidnapping complaint filed by a private detective from Montreal. He says you brought a child here. Can you tell me where she is?"

"Kidnapping! Surely, you must have the wrong house." Even as she spoke, the dead-serious look in the policeman's eyes told her he knew Ellie had been there. Marjorie's knees felt rubbery.

"Her father came for her at six forty-five. She went with him," Marjorie replied in a small voice. The policeman went to the back door and called out. A second officer emerged from the shrubbery.

Shaken, Marjorie stammered, "You put a guard on my back door before you rang the bell! What on earth is going on?"

"Don't worry, ma'am. We always do that."

The words of reassurance sent panic tingling through the nape of Marjorie's neck. *They know I took Ellie from the back of the condo. Surely they don't think I kidnapped her!*

"Mrs. Maynard, perhaps the fastest way to help the investigation would be for you to talk to the private detective. He's outside right now."

A third person approached the house—the same bull-necked man who had chased her down the highway.

"Mrs. Maynard, this is Mr. LeBlanc, from Montreal. Last night he came to us for help because he has no jurisdiction here."

Marjorie felt bewildered. He was no villain at all.

"I must say, Mrs. Maynard, you have excellent reflexes at the wheel of that car and quite a talent for evasion," the powerful man said, his face cold with sincerity. "You'd make a great moll for the Mafia."

Marjorie shrank from his condemnation. She wanted a new role in her life, but Mafia moll wasn't what she had in mind.

"Your Mr. Barker is no minister," said the detective. "He's a con artist, and Kate Darnell is not his wife. When she ran off with Barker, Ellie's father won custody of their daughter, Ellie. Barker kidnapped the little girl to help with his cover. They have been eluding the police and on the run ever since."

Marjorie didn't know what to say.

The policeman intervened. "Excuse me, Mr. LeBlanc, before you say any more, it seems Mrs. Maynard is acquainted with these people from the look on her face." Turning to Marjorie he continued. "It would be best if you came down to the station and gave the department a statement." Then he added something about apprehending the fugitives, a court case, and having a lawyer.

Marjorie's head reeled. She wasn't sure what the officer had said. She felt disoriented. *A statement—a lawyer—imagine, me needing a lawyer—what will Calvin say?* She must get dressed.

Transfixed in front of her closet, she realized she knew what to wear shopping or to the performing arts centre, but what did one wear to a police station? What if they took her picture, like a common criminal? The mint-green suit—that would look best.

The police had suggested five minutes for getting dressed. She finished in four with a minute left to make the two beds.

She could hear talking at the foot of the stairs. The police were still standing there! Did they think she would try to escape? Marjorie descended and turned towards the kitchen and garage. A policeman caught her arm.

"No, this way, Mrs. Maynard, the front door. We have a car waiting outside. We'll drive you to the station."

A blue-and-white patrol car now waited in the driveway. One of the officers walked ahead of her, and a second one followed. Marjorie felt mortified. She looked like a prisoner. She hardly knew the neighbours. What would they think, with the police taking her away? And the police—the police didn't seem to believe her. No one had ever doubted her honesty. How could she have been so stupid, so vulnerable, so easily fooled by Mr. Barker? He seemed so trustworthy. No wonder Calvin said that times had changed, that people were different from the old days! What was she to do? Her name would be associated with Barker in the newspapers. Calvin's business might suffer. All she wanted was to fulfill herself, and now the police suspected her of kidnapping a child.

❦

At the station, they took Marjorie to an interrogation room. She would have to stay at the station until they finished checking the condo.

They were nice enough. A policewoman brought coffee and offered to take her coat, but Marjorie could see that they took no chances. She heard the click of the door when it locked.

One detective warned her that, whether intentional or not, she was involved in the kidnapping—a serious felony if the court proved collusion with Barker.

Mr. LeBlanc smirked. "I bet he hasn't even paid you the first month's rent, Mrs. Maynard, if what you've told us is true," said the private investigator in a caustic tone. "I doubt that he'll be there when we raid the place."

She gave them a key to the condo and seated herself on the wooden chair.

A woman arrived with a portable typewriter. They wanted her statement. Marjorie had never dictated anything in her life. Giving the statement to the silent prissy-faced woman made Marjorie feel guilty. Her story might condemn her. How would she prove she was not privy to Mr. Barker's plans? And they insisted on the word "landlady." Had none of them ever heard the words "property manager"? Poor Calvin.

For another hour, Marjorie waited with the young policewoman supervising her incarceration. The officer tried to be pleasant, tried for congenial conversation, but Marjorie determined that she would not talk. What if they planted the officer to wheedle more information from her?

After an interminable wait, the police inspector arrived.

"Your Mr. Barker has gone. He and Kate, with little Ellie, have slipped by us again, but you'll be pleased to know that we've cleared you of suspicion. We know you were conned the same as his other victims because he took all of your furnishings, everything except the big sofa. He probably plans to sell them. I imagine he had them loaded in his panel truck when he came to your house at 6:45. I'm sure you're glad it's over, except of course if we need you to testify when we catch him. Thanks for your help."

She could go. She hoped they would use an unmarked car to drive her home, but the blue-and-white waited for her, and the polite young officer escorted her to her door. She dared not look up to see if any neighbours watched her arrival.

Gently, as if still afraid of making too much noise, Marjorie closed the door behind her, but it did not shut out her thoughts. She crossed the tiled floor of the entrance hall with its urn of dried flowers and looked around the elegant sitting room. Everything was in order. The pictures were straight, the footstool sat by the big chair, the pillows were puffed, music on the baby grand waited for a pianist. There was nothing left to do until Calvin arrived in a few hours, and when he did come and had heard her story, he would laugh. He would laugh about the condo and the money and say "Not to worry" to comfort her, as if nothing had been lost.

Where had she gone wrong? Why did she feel like such a failure when in many ways she had managed very well? Marjorie walked into the TV room and curled up under the blanket she had tucked over Ellie. *At least,* she told herself, *Mr. LeBlanc saw that I have talent, if only as a Mafia moll.*

V

SPRING SPECIAL

My first-year engineering classes were over, and I had a few days before my summer job started, so Gram decided to have a party with me as her butler. Gram is in her seventies, but the women on her guest list were older. She said she wanted me around in case any of them needed help. That sounded okay, plus a free meal, so I agreed.

The morning started on the cool side, but later the sun came out and warmed the day. I had my hair cut and laid my blue jeans aside in favour of a suit. I knew what Gram would expect. When I arrived early that afternoon, she had me setting up lawn chairs on the patio. This meant carrying half of the chairs from the basement, and every one needed dusting, with me in a black suit. That's when I took off my jacket and wished I'd ironed more than just the collar and cuffs of my white shirt, but Gram didn't say anything. I slid open the door to the patio, dragged the chairs outside, and had them looking perfect in no time.

Next, I filled a silver tray with eight old-fashioned glasses and washed and separated sprigs of mint for the mint juleps that she wanted me to serve. My tie got in the way, so I loosened the knot, lifted it over my head, and put it with my jacket on the dining room chair. I figured that I'd have time to put them on again when I finished making the drinks.

"Make the mint juleps just before the guests arrive," said Gram. "They must be fresh. The recipe is in that 'drinks' book on the counter."

Gram's kitchen had aromas better than any restaurant. When Gram put on a party, everyone knew that they were in for something special.

As directed, I counted twenty mint leaves into each old-fashioned glass. The book said, "Add two teaspoons of sugar and muddle till the sugar dissolves." To me, the word "muddle" didn't belong in a recipe. *It better not be me in a muddle* made its way into my thoughts.

I scanned the recipe for mint juleps. *Twenty mint leaves times eight mint juleps—that's one hundred and sixty mint leaves that have to look pretty dead.* "Fill glasses with crushed ice," I read on, "and pour bourbon over ice. Serve immediately." *They each get a whole glassful of bourbon? Whoops, I skipped a line.* "Two to three ounces of bourbon according to taste," it said. *What? I get to taste one of them?*

Gram started to welcome her guests. I thought, *Trapped in the kitchen in my unironed shirt, no tie, and no jacket, and the mint juleps aren't finished. Quick, line up the eight glasses on the counter, guess at two to three ounces of bourbon for the first glass, and fill 'em even.* I wondered what three ounces of bourbon looked like. I might as well give them a decent drink.

There's no time for tasting one. I wouldn't know what a good mint julep tasted like anyway.

A quick pass over all the glasses, and the mint juleps were ready, with the guests already out on the patio. *The dining room's empty. I'm saved!* I choked my tie up tight to the collar, swung into my jacket, and appeared at the patio door, tray in hand.

Gram beamed while I served each guest a mint julep. To me, every one of the guests came under the heading "quiet little old lady," but they laughed and talked as they sipped and had a great old time. Gram hadn't asked me to wash mint leaves for seconds, but seeing the drinks go down so fast, I slipped back into the kitchen and restarted the process. Mint leaves can be awfully wet when you're washing a bunch of them in a hurry, but I figured my shirt and jacket cuffs would dry. Could those old ladies ever laugh! If Gram wanted the bourbon to exercise their vocal chords, it sure worked. I could hear them from the kitchen, and I bet you could hear them down at Heinrick's Beer Garden.

The din grew stronger. I watched as they wobbled through the open patio door into the dining room. Gram had a wonderful selection of tasty cold-plate items on the buffet. Things quieted down while everyone filled their plates, seated themselves at the table, and ate half their lunch.

"What a lovely shrimp mousse, Grace," said Sadie. "As always, we're sure to remember the wonderful things we experience at your luncheons." Gram thanked Sadie for the compliment.

I think I saw it first—the top of the drape was wiggling, and it wasn't the wind.

"Grace, is that mousse with one 's' or two?" asked Mavis with a snicker.

"Mousse has two 'essess,' Mavis," said Gram. "Why do you ask?"

"Well," said Mavis with a great guffaw, "I think you've got one with *one* 's' doing acrobatics on the back of your drapes." Her explosion of raucous laughter threatened to teeter her backwards out of the chair.

The room went silent. The mouse swung from the end of the drapes to land with a thud on the top of the baby grand piano. It sat up and stared stupidly at the ladies, who by now had all sucked in their breath, prepared for fight or flight.

Gram looked at me as if catching the mouse was part of my job. I was thinking, *I guess I'll have to bash it into submission.* Having a club in my hand seemed like a good idea. I grabbed the fireplace poker.

I leapt into action, poker in hand, and went for the mouse on the piano. A lady, or maybe eight of them, shrieked in the background. This woke up the mouse, and it leapt onto the back of the sofa, which certainly saved the finish of Gram's piano from the poker. The mouse went under the cushion— *whap, whap*—out again, and over to the coffee table.

Soot on the poker! How could I smash the mouse using a blackened poker against Gram's lovely furniture? I dropped it and yanked off my shoe. *God, a hole in my sock!*

I didn't know that those old ladies had the strength to jump onto chairs in one leap—all but one that is, the one who first guffawed at the mouse. I figured that she'd caught mice before.

"I'll help you corner that varmint, son. It's under this overstuffed chair. Gimme your other shoe." I prayed that I wouldn't find a hole in my other sock, yanked off the shoe, and tossed it to her where she stood guarding the far side of the chair.

"I'll whack it," she said, "if it comes my way, and you have a go if it comes at you."

Good plan, I thought. It came, and I whacked, but the mouse ran back under the coffee table. *My whack failed.* My jacket restricted my movements. I ripped it off as I dashed for the mouse. I was too focused on catching the mouse to remember my unironed shirt. *Whap! Whap! Maybe I'd do better hitting with the heel of my shoe.*

Whoa! I had just caught the lamp from tipping over when the gal with my other shoe pushed past the coffee table. Out came the mouse. Bang went the heel of my shoe, right there on the coffee table.

A hush enveloped the room. *Oh, god. I've killed it!*

Eight sets of beady eyes levelled on me. Obviously, the ladies expected me to dispose of it. None of them offered to do the job. In my best nonchalant manner, I picked up the mouse by its grizzly little tail and did the first thing that came to mind. I opened the glass door of the fireplace and dropped it in there. I can remember giving the ladies a smile as if to say "That's the end of that" as I grabbed for my shoes and jacket and left to wash the guilt from my hands and get dressed again.

When I returned to the party, the ladies were seated and finishing their lunch. I could smell hair burning, but no one said anything. *Gram must have had the fireplace lit earlier and it held hot embers.* I guessed that the ladies were so old that they'd lost their sense of smell.

Then Mavis gave one of her famous guffaws again. Pointing at the fireplace, she said to me, "That varmint you whapped must have been a fat one. I can hear him sizzling in there."

Dead quiet.

When the ladies heard the sizzle, they whispered excuses to Gram and left. No one finished dessert. My odd sense of humour thought, *Gram always does serve something unique and tasty. This year's spring special—roast mouse served sizzling hot from the barbecue!*

VI

THE SHED –
A PERSONAL ESSAY

When the workmen started to demolish the shed standing behind our cottage on Coney Island, I went out to watch the demise of the building, over 100 years old. I thought that I could take a quick look and go back inside the cottage, but I couldn't. I watched the whole while as, wall by wall, the chainsaws ripped at its life. I stood there, alone, in the middle of the lawn watching, watching, my mind conjuring up the memories that the old shed pleaded to have someone remember. The roof, now leaking from holes chewed by squirrels, and the interior overrun with mice that gnawed holes in the floor and possibly spread hantavirus meant that the old shed had to go.

∽

At the turn of the century, The Northern Lumber Company owned the property along the beach of Safety Bay, Coney Island. In 1882, with nothing, William and Mary Shaw came from Liverpool to settle in Canada. Widowed in 1887, when her husband, a dining car employee, fell beneath the wheels of a Canadian Pacific train at Jackfish Bay, Lake Superior, Mary Shaw rejected the idea of returning to Liverpool. It offered nothing for a person with no skills. Determined to make her way as a settler in this handsome, wild country, Mary Shaw practised midwifery when there was no doctor. Throughout the town, she cared for the ill and the elderly as a housemother when a family needed help. Soon everyone knew her as Auntie Shaw. In the early days, she bought a small rowboat so she could row over to Coney Island for picnics and campouts, just to enjoy nature.

⚭

Before the turn of the century, during the summers the lumber company stored sleeping shacks, built on skids, along Auntie Shaw's favourite stretch of beach. In the winter these shacks were hauled down the lake on the ice by teams of horses for the lumberjacks to use. Out in the wilderness, the shacks afforded some protection while the men cut trees and dragged the logs onto the ice to form log booms. When the lake melted in the spring, the log booms were towed by tugboat downstream to the lumber mill in Kenora, and again the shacks were beached on Coney Island before the ice went out.

For ten years, despite the lumber company's shacks, Mary Shaw continued to spend many summer weekends on the beaches of Safety Bay. She knew that she had made the right decision—a decision that offered her a better way of life than Liverpool in the 1890s. In 1897, she invited her niece, Sarah Elizabeth Knipe, to follow her to Canada from Liverpool. She wanted her niece to enjoy the freedom that she herself found in the New World.

Elizabeth left the dreary streets of Liverpool to live with her Aunt Mary, who came to be a second mother to her. After three years, Lil, as she was known, met and married Alfred Edward Hargrave, also a railroader, for Kenora was a divisional point for the C.P.R. They raised their first three children in Kenora with Nana, as the children called Mary Shaw.

The lumber company moved into other areas and sold the land on Safety Bay to a land developer in Kenora. In the winter of 1913, he subdivided the land into lots. Auntie Shaw gathered up her meagre savings and rushed to buy property on her "favourite beach." With spring breakup, Mary Shaw, my husband's great great-aunt, immediately rowed over to Coney to inspect the lot she now owned. To her amazement, she found a lumberjack shack abandoned on the beach of her lot.

The ten by twelve foot shack meant that she owned a summer home as well as property! The building had simple, thin walls, but its construction on the heavy skids made it a prize find. With the help of her niece and nephew-in-law, Lil and Al Hargrave, and their three children, Marion, Bill and Hamer, plus others, she pulled the shack to the back of the beach, and she set up her "camp," as the locals still call their cottages to this day. For indeed, they were camping. The whole family used the shack as a change house. Meals came from a campfire. If the weather became inclement and the boys' tent intolerable, bedrolls on the floor of the shed pressed against each other like Nana's rising biscuits.

Lean-to additions were added to the shed for a kitchen, a porch, and other bedrooms. With these additions, the original shed became Auntie Shaw's bedroom and chief support for the additions.

World War I ended. The Hargrave children grew up.

When electricity came to the island, Auntie Shaw's bedroom glowed at night from one open light bulb dangling on a cloth-encased double-twisted wire hanging from the ceiling. Stories tell that Auntie Shaw thrilled at the sight of the new electric installation. I visualized the picture I'd seen of my husband's Aunt Betty, born years later in 1918, being held by Auntie Shaw as she rocked her great-niece to sleep under that light.

The near wall fell to the chainsaws. I could see the wired socket still dangling lifelessly from the ceiling. I watched it swing as the chainsaws dropped it into the rubble.

As I stood there the relentless chainsaws chewed through another wall and the wallpaper that adorned it. I knew that Auntie Shaw had wallpapered the interior of the shack in its early years, first with newspaper, using flour paste, and then with wallpaper samplers, to keep out drafts and to enhance the rough walls. In and out, as the men cut around each supporting two-by-four and corner post, the wallpaper clung to the end. Somehow, while the chainsaws shredded through the wallpaper, a scrap of yellowed newspaper blew free from the riddled wallpaper and fluttered to my feet, as if willed by the shed to have me read it. Amazing! The three-inch scrap of newspaper came from a corner of a paper showing the date. It read 1916.

⁓

In these magnificent surroundings of wild greenery, I imagined the family gatherings in those early days. I smelled the bacon frying, the scent of coffee wafting on the air during the hot days of summer, with meals cooked out-of-doors on a grate supported over an open fire. After the kitchen lean-to was added and graced with a wood-burning cookstove, the family cooked indoors only in May and September when the air chilled the bones or when it rained—they liked camping on an open fire.

ᶜᣞᣛᣞᣙ

As the shed lost its doorframe to the chainsaws, I remembered a black-and-white snapshot of the early twenties. It pictured my mother-in-law to be, Marion, the eldest child, and her brother, Hamer, with a guitar in his lap, on the doorstep of the old camp. While the chainsaws shrilled, I heard the strains of "The Charleston," vibrant with the fun of post-war music.

I remembered the stories of Boxing Day when the Hargraves and Auntie Shaw visited during the winter. The family would snowshoe across the ice to Coney Island, heat up the potbellied stove in Auntie Shaw's room, and enjoy Christmas leftovers after skating on a patch of lake ice that they had shovelled free of drifted snow.

Now I could see a corner post of the shed laid bare. On it, near the roof, I saw a familiar angled nail. I had seen it before at the top of the post and knew its story. In these final minutes of life, the nail seemed to be clinging to the memory of the times when, to celebrate the holidays, it held the ends of red and green crepe-paper streamers that were strung across the interior of the shed's pitched roof.

The camp came to Lil Hargrave on Auntie Shaw's passing in 1928. In 1935, Al and Lil built the present cedar-log camp. All of the additions on the old camp were scrapped except Auntie Shaw's bedroom, the old shed on skids. Come-alongs yanked the shed to a spot directly behind the new camp. Cedar shingles on the roof and walls improved the shed's appearance. Everything that the family did not want to store in their new camp went into the shed—Al's carpentry and garden tools, fishing gear, and the big saw used for cutting blocks of ice to be stored in the icehouse built at the back of the property.

In Grandpa's big wooden boat with a Ford motor in its hold, my husband, then a boy of nine, helped his grandpa, Al Hargrave, to bring slabs of slate from Slate Island to the camp for a sidewalk out to the shed.

⟜∞⟞

All of Al and Lil Hargrave's grandchildren grew up going to this camp in the summer when they were little, but somehow the other grandchildren went their own ways while my husband and I and our four sons came every year to help out as his grandparents grew older. The new camp had a refrigerator, and the eyesore of an icehouse was demolished.

⟜∞⟞

In 1972, our boys were becoming teenagers and needed more space. We invited the neighbours along the beach to help move the shed to the bush at the back of the lot so we could build a sleeping shack close to the camp. With the shed's original construction on skids, the gang of men rolled it, back wall leading, over the lawn on boom logs. Every few feet a log was removed from the grass at the front door of the shed and positioned ahead of the moving building as they made progress down the lawn. This gang of twelve or so set the shed up on prepositioned supporting posts. The fellows consumed the case of beer and my husband levelled the shed by rolling an empty beer bottle on its battleship-grey painted floor. We continued to use "the shed"—its official name—for storing gasoline, paint, gardening equipment, an old trunk with Auntie Shaw's treasures, and some logging tools.

Earlier in the week, as I emptied the shed, ready for the demolition crew, I knew I would find the logging tools used in the early days and the trunk, for I had saved them from being cast off forty years earlier. Carefully, I cleaned and oiled three tremendous saws—a buck saw, a Swedish saw, and the long saw with nasty looking teeth, used for cutting the blocks of ice out of the lake some 100 years earlier. There were also two tools for working the log booms and two for hunting small wild animals. At some time in the past Grandpa used all of these tools.

The workmen cut the walls of the shed in slabs like stretchers, piled them neatly in stacks of four, and carried them off to the waiting barge just as soldiers would be carried off the fields of war by medics. Stretcher after stretcher carried away pieces of the shed in a way that, to me, seemed fitting, as if the old warrior of a shed still deserved some dignity.

The crew took away every last shred of evidence and raked the plot clean. I could not believe how emotional I felt about the shed's complete disappearance.

Later this year a new shed blossomed on that same site. Inside we placed Auntie Shaw's old trunk, still guarding her treasures. None of us wanted them disturbed. It held a wedding gift of 1882—a coffee service of beautifully sculpted pewter, complete with the coffeepot, cream pitcher, sugar bowl and a little tray, all in perfect condition. When Mary Shaw left Liverpool with her husband, William, to go off to Canada, someone must have given her the large embroidered shawl of natural silk, bearing the words "Forget Me Not" set above finely stitched flowers. With this bundle lay a white embroidered and tatted christening gown, likely the one used for my husband's mother in 1901, and a 1920s sleek white cotton petticoat, all in excellent condition. The final bundle held priceless old photos. The property had lost the old shed to the ravages of nature, but surely these treasures, along with the logging tools, would sustain our memories of the past just as the shed had done for so long.

∽∞∾

Perhaps this story isn't all that interesting, but the shed had a lively background. I felt that its story must be recorded so that future generations of our family would know the early history of this delightful property on a beach of Coney Island, Lake of the Woods, Kenora, Ontario. I want them to know why the handsome new building at the back of the lot is simply called "the shed." Six generations knew the old shed. No wonder I had to stand and watch its passing.

VII

KINSHIP

Propped at the window of my townhouse, I am ready for the morning parade to start. First to come will be Mrs. Fyfe from the unit two doors down, then the new lady from 148, and finally poker-faced Pomeroy with Boswell, his boxer. One by one, they will pass my window with their dogs, all headed for the dog run at the end of the condos, despite the cheerless weather. They will not keep me waiting; they never do. I often wonder just who keeps whom so regular in their habits.

Here they come. Mitzy, the apricot poodle, straining at her leash, has old Mrs. Fyfe bobbing along in her wedgies, tethered by the right hand. Her left hand clutches at the collar of her fine wool coat to ward off the wind that tousles her apricot-tinted permed curls. Down the street the sprightly apricot duo mince together, their toes turned out, as the poodle breed is known to do.

Number 148 is next on the scene. She has a white polo coat with large black buttons. The coat has a black collar, just like her dog. I have no doubt that the lady has a name, but it takes a while to learn such things from behind a pane of glass. Certainly, she is punctual and very determined, judging from the look of her sturdy walking shoes. I always notice shoes. They tell so much about a person. There she goes, stride for stride, with her Dalmatian—two racers in black and white, striking a direct line through the light skiff of snow as the dog pulls her over the curbs and parking stalls at the entrance of the dog run. It crosses my mind that she needs the dogged determination and the sinewy limbs of an Olympic runner to match the dog's pace, lest her tether should rip off her arm at the shoulder.

And now for Boswell, the boxer, checking out each lamp standard, as is his custom while his servant, Mr. Pomeroy, warm in his black boots, dutifully waits at the end of his leash with each pause for identification. Mr. Pomeroy's lean jowls are protected from the cold by his short black beard, barely distinguishable at the collar from his leather coat, as shiny and black as Boswell's. There they stand as if posing for a study in still life that I would title "The Mating Game."

None of them notice me at my window. None of them know that they brighten my day, but as usual, when "Boz" and Pomeroy inspect my lamppost, I see two matching jowled faces and, in their eyes, as with the others, a kinship of long understanding. And I chuckle as I gaze at the heavy wool socks on my feet and wonder what breed of dog I resemble and if such a kinship could train my wheelchair and me to go walking.

VIII

THE OTHER SIDE
OF THE WORLD, 1980S

Tears welled in my eyes as I realized what I held in my hand—two unexpected letters together in one envelope, one from Namir and the other one from Margaret, with no return address. Raising my eyes, unfocused, to the view through my front window, instead of seeing the winter sun highlighting smooth fields of snow, I imagined a tropical sun on hot desert sand. Life in the Middle East seemed only yesterday, but the calendar told me that twelve busy months had slipped by since my return to the Canadian prairies.

Scenes of that morning when I first met Margaret flooded my brain as one unbidden thought after another tumbled into my consciousness. Again I sensed the first light of dawn on that eventful day, and I felt my feet brush the soft carpet as I made my way to the kitchen to fetch an early morning coffee.

Although my hands still clutched the letters, my right hand paused, outstretched above the kitchen water faucet, with my mind in overdrive. Slowly my thoughts played back scene after scene as that first uneasy day presented itself.

∽✺∾

Through my early morning stupor, there beyond the kitchen window that faced onto the servants' courtyard I saw a slender bronze hand release the bathroom doorknob and disappear inside. The hand of a woman? Impossible!

I rubbed the sleep from my eyes and concentrated on my view of the servants' quarters. Adrenalin surged through my body. My thoughts focused. Seven a.m. Sunday, Namir's day off. I had to be imagining things, but I couldn't deny what I had seen. Namir had a woman in his room!

For two years, Namir had worked as our houseboy and lived in the attached servants' quarters at the back of the house in the Middle East. I trusted him, a Muslim from India and a bachelor. Surely he knew the penalty for having a woman!

I drew back the hand poised to twist the cold water tap. If I turned on the water to make coffee, he'd hear it in the pipes and sense my presence watching his quarters. Silently, I altered the angle of the slats in the Venetian blind to hide me from view, and I watched the empty courtyard, determined to know more. Sooner or later someone had to appear.

As I waited, I worried. My mind teemed with related thoughts. *Middle East countries follow Muslim law; Muslim men cannot date or fraternize with a woman before marriage— my god, the police might come at any moment if he's been reported to the authorities—he could be stoned to death if caught with a woman, and we could be deported for being involved with him. How can Namir say prayers five times a day and do such a thing?* None of the pieces in the puzzle fit.

Minutes melted away under the relentless morning sun. I stared across the courtyard through the narrow slats and the window's metal burglary grill. The courtyard was walled on four sides, with a servants' gate in one corner. The two green doors on the opposite wall remained shut, one hiding the person in the bathroom and the other, no doubt, shielding Namir from view. Nothing moved in the shimmering heat, not one beetle or a windblown petal from the neighbour's purple bougainvillaea. My bare feet chilled on the cold terrazzo floor, but I watched every second. I had to determine how much danger we were in.

Why now, with my husband out of town? And the Arab authorities—will they speak to me or only to my husband? Had they seen her arrive? I waited like a hawk, my focus glued to the stretch of wall between the two doors.

A figure flitted from the bathroom back to Namir's room. My eyes had not deceived me earlier; I saw a slim, graceful woman wrapped in a bedsheet, her long black hair shining wet like satin as it dripped against her smooth bronze shoulders.

Get dressed. Confront them. She must not leave by the servants' gate—too many Muslim eyes in our compound. No one must know that Namir had a woman last night.

At that moment, I realized that I'd chosen loyalty and trust over Muslim law in trying to protect my servant from his ignorance, indiscretion, or disobedience. Whatever his reason, I knew I couldn't turn him in to the authorities. With no one to turn to for advice and the moments slipping away, I found myself embarking on a plan of deceit in the eyes of the local government. If I failed, we would all go down together.

Namir answered my knock, his cherubic face solemn. He made no denials. In the privacy of the courtyard, he gently led his guest into the open. To my surprise, she wore a simple skirt and blouse, not an Indian sari or Arabic costume. She forced her eyes to meet my gaze. I saw fear and desperation in those black-brown pools. She looked to be thirty, about the same age as Namir; perhaps she'd been beautiful at twenty-five, but she was aging quickly.

"Madam," he said, according to his people's custom with employers. "Madam, this is Margaret, a friend of my aunt. Margaret is a Christian from Sri Lanka and has no place to go." Namir had practised what he would say. I could tell by the stiff quality of his diction and the worry lines across his forehead below his crown of wavy brown hair.

That explained the skirt and blouse. It hadn't occurred to me that a Christian servant from a former British colony would be as identifiable by her clothing as other people in town were by theirs, for everyone wore their national costume. From the style and prestige of clothes one could guess national origin and how people were employed, for work permits seemed to be issued by country. Baluchi labourers, middle-class Indian shopkeepers, low-caste Indian house servants, Pakistani taxi drivers, Sikh tradesmen, European and North American oil experts—all wore different outfits, with the Arab men in their white robes and their women in black.

In the windless courtyard, under the glare of the desert sun, Namir made his case, not knowing if it would cost him his job, maybe his life, but honest with me to the end. I realized that he had nowhere else to turn for help. It seemed that he wanted me to catch them together because he trusted me. I smiled, and he knew the three of us had a pact of secrecy.

I went to the gate to be sure no witness would see us cross to the kitchen door, then led the frightened woman and Namir into the cool of the house.

"Can you sew?"

My demand surprised her. "Yes, Madam, and cook. In Sri Lanka, I kept a nice home. My husband worked as a chief accounting clerk." Her eyes fell to her hands with embarrassment. "Well, that is, until he ran away with his secretary and left me and our two children with all the bills and no money. I had no training for a job, and in the custom of Sri Lanka, my position and education made it impossible for me to be a servant. No one would hire me." She paused and proudly raised her head. "My two children and I were starving, so I signed a contract to come here for work where no one would know me."

I interrupted her story. "Namir, close the dining room drapes and open the sewing machine on the table in there, then go to your room and pack everything of Margaret's into a bag and bring it in here. Your room must be clear." The urgency in my voice sent him off at a run.

Namir returned in minutes to find a length of cloth on the table with a pattern pinned to it. I turned to Margaret. "We can't be sure if the neighbours have seen something or that you weren't followed last night by the foot patrol. No one on the compound knows I own a sewing machine. With this setup, a visitor will think I've hired you to make me some clothes. If the doorbell rings, work at the sewing. It doesn't matter if you waste the cloth. No matter who might arrive, a good friend or otherwise, I'll tell them that I borrowed you from my American friend in the city."

With our cover in place, my urgency receded. "How is it, Margaret, that you have nowhere to go?"

"In Sri Lanka," she answered, "there is a company that ships maids out of the country on three-year contracts. Fifty of us travelled here under a group work permit and were employed in the houses assigned to us. In exchange for full-time service, we were to have a room and meals, with a new dress and two hundred dirhams each month."

Two hundred dirhams, I thought. *Namir gets eight hundred dirhams a month for just two hours of work each day, but no meals. Margaret is underpaid.*

A sharp knock at the door resounded through the house. Margaret cowered. I pushed her toward the sewing machine and answered the door. Little Badia, the neighbour's daughter, gave me a big smile and explained in simple English that her ball had bounced over our wall into the garden.

I led her past Margaret to the sliding door in the dining room and motioned for her to find her ball. Margaret concentrated on each snip of the scissors.

When Badia returned with her ball, her eyes inspected every room possible as she made her way to the front door. Before leaving, she turned for one last look, held up the ball, and smiled her thanks. Arab children seldom played in the street, and Badia had never come to my door before. Was she sent by her parents on a mission to prove a suspicion, or did she just happen to lose her ball?

I joined Margaret at the table, and she continued her story. "I've been working for an Egyptian family here in town for a year. My children are with my parents in Sri Lanka. Before I left, I found a one-room house in a poor part of Colombo where they could live together. My parents are old, with very little money of their own, but the two hundred dirhams I earn each month is sent by the company to keep them."

Hardly enough for four people, I calculated, and Margaret would have nothing.

Margaret continued, "My employers were fair, according to the contract, but after three months I didn't need any more dresses. I would rather have had a little money for writing paper. I suggested the change, but my madam insisted that the company must have had good reasons when they set the terms of the contract, and she refused to make any changes. They had six children. I worked all hours and every day."

What a job, I thought. But still, she had signed the contract, so it must have been better than she could do in Sri Lanka. But why had Margaret no place to go?

Namir made tea, and we moved to the kitchen table. Margaret went on, "My Egyptian family was transferred. The company decided to put me with a national family, and I was afraid." She sighed and went on softly. "I feared abuse. The men in this country can have four wives. Some are used to having many women. I knew he would think me lowly for being a Christian—might expect me to fulfill his sexual whims. The night before my Egyptians left, I ran away rather than be transferred to a local national's home."

I knew that running away occurred among poorly paid domestic help. It seemed the only way to survive when faced with a choice between intolerable working conditions and deportation, with no job back home. The necessary false papers for a work permit could easily be purchased from unscrupulous sources.

So that was it; Namir wanted me to find Margaret a job with one of my friends who had accommodations for a servant. Surely I could find her a better paying job with a free day for herself! What degradation and hard work the poor woman had endured to protect and provide for her children. How she missed them; a letter every few months, she said. To protect Namir and ourselves, I had to be careful whom I asked in finding work for her.

"How did you arrive at Namir's room?" I asked.

Again her story touched my heart. She had hidden under the hibiscus bushes of a park the first night and then begged breakfast in the early morning light from an Indian woman going to market who she guessed was a maid. The woman had been kindly and took her back to her quarters. For three days, the woman risked hiding Margaret and fed her while they decided what to do.

Namir took up the story. "That woman is my aunt. She works at Al Qattans' here on the compound." I had met Namir's Aunt Zahra. She had servants' quarters identical to ours—a single room with a separate bathroom. Her husband lived with her but worked out of town in the oil fields during the week.

Namir went on, "When my uncle, Ismail, came in for the weekend, they were much crowded, and Ismail was afraid Al Qattans would see Margaret and turn them all over to the police, so he said she must go. In the dark last night, I brought her here."

Namir's courage and decency towards another human being in trouble impressed me. Muslim law or not, he recognized her desperation.

Namir worked for other households as well as ours—one of them our American friends. Their home had a room behind the kitchen intended for servants' quarters. It measured two metres by two metres, literally a hard bunk with an aisle beside it.

"Namir, pack a few things and move into the servants' room at Danby's house. You'll have to live there until I find a job with quarters for Margaret. You'll go to jail or worse if they find you two together. And put a drape over your window before you leave. Do you know how to get Margaret some papers?"

"My aunt, she did that."

Such a turmoil they must have felt these past few days, hiding Margaret from Zahra's Muslim household. False papers usually cost five hundred dirhams, likely all their savings! My efforts paled beside their generosity to a stranger, a Christian, when their helping her might bring the law down on them.

During the next few days, I found Margaret a job on the compound. She moved out of Namir's room. He came home, and I breathed a sigh of relief. We had done it.

⁓

Sunday afternoon, Margaret arrived at my front door. "Madam, I came to thank you for protecting me and to ask permission to see Namir. According to your wishes, I came to your front door rather than be seen at the servants' gate. My new madam has given me the day off, and I don't know what to do with it." Her old-fashioned English reflected her schooling. No doubt Sri Lankan schools still used old Victorian books, shipped from Britain in colonial times.

"Go for a walk along the ocean. Go to the market. There's lots of things you can do," I rattled on as I led her through the house to the kitchen door.

"Where is the ocean, madam? I have never seen an ocean in this city. My Egyptian family took me to a store only twice to carry packages for madam."

In one year, had she never been to the ocean or walked along the corniche, a lovely paved drive with its elegant sea wall and palm trees all along the beaches of the city? Had she never been downtown to wander in the colourful outdoor markets or seen the beautiful minareted mosques and their gardens? She didn't know of the fascinating jewellery stores, their windows heavy with yellow gold? How caged she must have felt. Now things would be better. With her Western employer, she would have more money to send home and some money and time to herself.

"Namir, Margaret is here," I called softly from the kitchen door. "She's never been downtown. If she is to survive, you must teach her how to use a taxi without getting cheated." To Margaret, "There are no bus routes. Everyone travels by taxi; it's the only way."

꧁◎꧂

I remembered my first taxi ride. The taxis had no meters, and we had forgotten to settle the price for the ride in advance. The taxi driver guessed we were newcomers to the country and raised the price. He demanded one hundred dirhams. My husband gave him twenty-five dirhams and a scowl and stepped from the cab. To our horror, the driver chased us down the street, his Baluchi pants and shirttail flapping, his grey beard frothed with saliva.

"Polize! Polize!" he yelled as we dodged a local who lunged at us. We had an appointment with the sales manager for Honda cars. The manager, seeing the commotion, came to our rescue by stepping out on the street to confront the taxi driver while we slipped into the salesroom.

"You were an easy mark, my friend," said the sales manager when he returned. "You paid twenty-five dirhams for a three-dirham ride. He figured if you were that stupid, he could make more. Don't think of it as cheating you. It is the Eastern way. In your country you call it *buyer beware,* but here, they are more *enthusiastic* in its practice. You will soon learn your values. And, my friend, you must always laugh when you bargain with a vendor who quotes too high a price.

That lets him laugh too, and he can try a lower price without losing face. It's all a game to them."

꿍

Margaret often came to our door in the following month. One evening at dusk, I heard her voice in Namir's room. She had used the servants' gate! I would speak to him in the morning. The risk was too great. Only the day before, the radio reported a modern-day stoning in another part of the country for pre-marital fraternity. A public whipping bloodied the woman's back until she collapsed, and the man, staked to the ground for a stoning execution, met death from a truckload of gravel dumped over him.

"Namir, as a Muslim bachelor, you are taking too great a risk. You are putting us all at risk. Surely Margaret can manage on her own now. You should stop seeing her."

"Madam, we are very careful. I wear the black pants and white shirt you gave me for serving table. They are Christian clothes to match Margaret's, and we bought a ring for her to wear. It makes us safe when we walk together in town."

"But what future is there in it, Namir?"

I should have known that his lilting singsong answer would rationalize the seriousness of the situation. "Madam, I have no future until I save money enough to give my sister in India a big dowry. In my country a man will not marry unless his woman comes with money enough for house furniture. I cannot marry until my sister marries, as my father is dead and I must fill his role. In two years I will have money enough for her dowry. In the meantime, Margaret needs me."

How dare he continue to put us at risk when I'd saved him from exposure and had been so patient? My irritation rose to the surface. "Why is that, Namir? Why does Margaret need you?"

"Madam, you wouldn't understand. When you go in town, your type clothes, the way you walk and buy things, everyone knows you are the wife of an American—well, Canadian; it's the same to them. You have power, and they leave you alone. When Margaret goes in town alone, she has no power. Her skirt and blouse, her looks, her little money, tells them she is a poor Sri Lankan, a Christian servant. The men in the market bump her and feel her. They cheat in giving change. For all her misery, she was safer working for the Egyptians, where she stayed inside. The contract writer in Sri Lanka knew what would happen. He knew best."

Namir continued, "And don't think she could dress like a Muslim lady to escape their abuse. It wouldn't help. Young Muslim women do not go in town alone. You see us by your ways, not ours, or the Arabs.' We are all different, but don't worry. With me dressing like a Christian husband, I can care for her. We won't get caught. When we have saved money enough, we will each go back to our countries and families. We are like sister and brother, very careful."

The two years planned to save enough money would likely stretch to four, maybe more. I felt sure of it. Could they last that long, fooling the authorities? Every day made Namir's crime worse. Could he rationalize Muslim prayers and parade as a Christian in the market? Were they, as he said, like brother and sister, or were they in love?

There seemed no way to resolve their problems. I felt that he and Margaret must have rehearsed what he planned to say, ready for the day when I tried to intervene, for with Margaret's help his English had improved immeasurably. With such dedication, there was little more I could say to stop them. He seemed determined to protect Margaret on her trips to the market.

Slowly, I perceived the differences in cultures. For me, she had been degraded and underpaid. For her and Namir, life brought many risks, and she could survive here better than she had in Sri Lanka. In the eyes of the Arab government, her actions were illegal—she was not working at the job as a maid that her group work permit allowed. Each in our own way had a point. They would no more recognize my point of view than I did theirs; it was not our cultural way. Their ideas would stand miles apart from mine, no matter where any of us lived, and nothing would likely change us—neither the Arabs, Namir and Margaret, nor me.

❧

Three months after Margaret came into our lives, in November, we were transferred back to Canada. When we arrived, I sent them a Christmas card, addressed to my American friend. Now, a year later, the blue envelope had arrived with two letters. Neat round writing filled two pages. I felt sure that the spelling of every word had been checked in the dictionary that I had given Namir for his birthday.

Once again, I read, "May God Bless You Two" written at the top of both sheets of lined white paper. I turned to Margaret's letter and started to read.

> *Dear Madam and Boss,*
> *Thank you very much for your kindness of sending us*
> *a letter. I never expected you to think of us again. Just*
> *after you left, I received a letter two months old saying*
> *that my twelve-year-old girl had been hit by a car and*

was in a coma. I borrowed the money to go to her. She survived, but it took me four months to get back here. My madam gave away the job you found me and my quarters, so now I work for a national family on the other side of town with poor money. Namir lives far away. I see him only once a week or two. And I am very sorry to see him like he is, because as you might have guessed, we are close to each other. He is living in your same villa. After you left, the lady who came was not good with Namir and not kind. Namir was very unhappy, but because of the room, he worked for her until they were transferred out again. Now there is another family. We shall see. Really, Madam, we will never find a family like you, a kind-mind lady. We will never forget you, and we are thanking you for your kindness. May God bless you forever. As for me and Namir, we have our health and each other, do not worry for us.
Yours faithfully, Margaret.

Namir wrote,

Dear Madam and Boss,
Every week now I have only two part-time hourlies and no good pay. I hope that you are well and how are your childrens. All our love to Madam and Boss and bless you. Pardon me Sir that you can see many wrongs in our letters. Madam, you know that we don't have good knowledge.
Yours affectionately, Namir.

Since my departure, their world had crumbled. They were barely surviving, yet there was no complaining. They were thankful to have their health and each other.

As I gazed across the fields covered with snow, with all my heart I tried to think as they would think, and I bowed my head and prayed for their continued good fortune.

IX

DYING FOR DINNER

With exotic movements propounding her grace and elegance, Margot starts across the dance floor as if heading for the small table in the shadowed corner of the dining room. Kaleidoscope lights above the empty dance floor play on her strawberry-blonde hair and reflect from the sequins of her black dress. With each gyration of her slim body, her solo crossing of the dance floor could have aroused the hordes of Babylon, but the men in the dining room continue with their business conversations, unmoved. How can men eating alone be more interested in their steaks than in a beautiful woman? Just three rows of tables separate Margot from the table in the corner. She must score soon.

Pause and pretend you are looking for someone, her conscience tells her.

Candlelight radiates through the dining room, highlighting the dinner guests against rose-coloured table linens and polished oak-panelled walls. Quiet conversation blends with soft music. Nothing resembles the pizza parlours Margot can afford. She feels like she has stepped onto a revolving stage and rotated into the wrong set. Where is the director? What is her cue? It isn't like drama school at all. If she's an actress, why doesn't she feel like acting? It's all a mistake. She shouldn't have come.

In desperation, she clutches her small handbag. It reminds her that all the money she has left is two dollars and fifty-nine cents. If her plan for picking up a free meal doesn't work, she'll have to choose between soup and a bus fare to the hostel.

What have you got to lose? The management can only throw you out. Surely, a summer with the Young Canadians and four years of drama school have taught you something. Come on, Mugs, you can do it. Toss your golden hair and smile.

She passes between the tables in the first row along the far edge of the dance floor. *What does it take to rouse these drones, sitting here in their dark suits with ties that label them as members of the establishment, successful and confident of their ability in the business world? Aren't any of them lonely when away from home? What more do I have to do to make them desire my company? I need dinner! Move toward that table with the single occupant and smile. Smile, or he'll guess you're hungry.* He chews vacantly on another pork rib.

It's so long since she's last eaten that a chiropractor could have done a spinal adjustment on her from the front, but she smiles.

She has tried being a shop clerk, to earn extra money, but the work interferes with tryouts. Waitressing is no better. Who needs an actress with rough hands? Desperation and hunger have pulled her to Granville to try to cadge a meal from Vancouver's elite. If she can get through the night, she is sure tomorrow will bring a role in live theatre, a TV commercial, or some modelling to keep her dream of acting alive. Others have made it; why not her?

She slows her pace to match the rhythm of the music—only one table between her and the table in the corner. *God, how many parts do you have to wiggle?* she thinks as she makes eye contact with the glazed orbs of an older man wearing a diamond tie tack. His straight-line pasted-on smile continues to simper. Nothing there but cobwebs. It's the booze. If the fools drank less, their hormones might work better.

Her plan is not working. She has crossed all of the distance between the small table in the corner and the French doors behind her leading to the front foyer. No one has patted her bum or tweaked a thigh. How can she start up a conversation if no one notices her?

Whores in the bar on the other side of the foyer fair better, but she can't expect to nab supper by mingling with them. You can't even sit at the bar if you haven't the price of a beer. And the men! The men that come on in the bar aren't looking for the same kind of a meal that she has in mind.

On the other hand, maybe she should make one pass through their territory. It might work, and if it doesn't, she can always come back to her first plan and saunter between the tables toward this one in the back corner. She pretends she has just remembered something, turns, and slips out of the dining room.

Across the foyer of the restaurant is the bar. She pauses at the swinging doors and looks in at the crowd. The loud rock beat of the music and the raucous chatter isn't like the hotel bar in Thorsby. Where are Alberta's bronze-faced farmers with their pearl-buttoned cowboy shirts and huge Stetsons? Where is the Saturday night disk jockey with his pulsating country music, or a friendly voice calling her to join the gang in a game of darts and a cool pint?

Thorsby seems a long time ago. Her mind allows hometown scenes to flip through her head—high school queen, Rosalind in *As You Like It,* voted most likely to succeed as an actress. After graduation from drama school, a role in Edmonton's Fringe Festival that summer, and then—nothing. She remembers the lonely bus ride that brought her to the bright lights of Vancouver and her resolve to become a star. After a year of making the circuits looking for work, her bank account was empty. Now, two months later, her health is showing the strain. She blocks this thought out and lifts her chin.

Everyone counts on me to put Thorsby on the map. They need something to raise their spirits, and grain prices sure aren't going to do it. I've got to succeed. I just have to—and she strolls into the bar.

Her slim black sheath with the sequins isn't right. It doesn't go with the men's jeans and designer T-shirts, the women's short, tight skirts and ribbed tops.

She hears, "Hey, guys, here's a new one."

Another man's voice calls out, "Stick it to 'em, Lola."

A third shouts, "Yo, baby! Now that's class!"

Margot realizes that they are raising their Coors to her. It is not the kind of recognition she wants. The crowd parts in front of her, allowing a pathway to a bar stool next to three leggy vamps.

Whores! They think I am one of them.

The nearest of the painted women slips from her stool and approaches with a candy-sweet smile, then spits in Margot's face. "My territory, girlie," the whore growls.

As Margot wipes away the spittle, the crowd cheers for the ladies to mix it up in a brawl. She ducks the woman's venomous talons. A ring forms around Margot and the whore. The patrons chant for more action. Luckily the whore has had too many beers to manage the stiletto heels she is sporting. She staggers backwards. Amid rock beats and laughter, the whore wobbles an ankle this way and that and clutches at manly shoulders. With her attacker claiming centre stage, Margot uses the right moves to slip through the crowd and out of the bar as if on cue.

The cool air of the foyer chills her shoulders. She feels drained, beaten, hungry. If only the two dollars and fifty-nine cents were more.

What are you made of, Mugs? You can't let a few catcalls unnerve you. You can still go back to the dining room, pesters her conscience.

She stands alone in the foyer, half dazed from hunger, and allows jumbled thoughts to tumble through her head again.

"Mugs," that's what people in Thorsby called her. They'd laugh at her pretentious "Margot." Mugs is short for Margaret, but movie stars are never named Margaret! Years ago, in dancing class, she used to pretend she was Margot Fonteyn to gain a psychological edge in dancing competitions. It is easy to think of herself as Margot instead of Margaret. The make-believe name gives her confidence. It feels right when she is with other actors.

⁓

Once more her conscience needles her. *Quit stalling, Mugs. Margot wouldn't give in. Try the dining room.*

As Margot stands in the hallway gathering her courage, a male hand from nowhere catches her elbow. Reflex tells her to run—his outfit is too slick—but maybe he is her supper ticket. Where's her mettle? She *is* an actress, isn't she? Time to turn on the charm until they'd eaten and then do the old washroom disappearing act if he had other ideas.

He's clearing his throat. He's going to speak. Time to flash her green eyes in his direction.

"Listen sister, yer crowdin' my territory, crashin' my line-up. Know what I mean?" a gravel voice drones in her ear. His casual grip has shifted to clamp deftly over a nerve in her upper arm with excruciating pain as he propels her toward the door. "Now, if you insist on hangin' around here, I'll be happy to add ya to my stable, but I got rules. Ya gotta do what I sez, or yer finished. Like into a dumpster!"

*Their pimp. You've landed their pimp. Play it cool, or you'll be labelled a prostitute for life. Improvise! You've got to ditch him on **your** terms!* She lowers her eyebrows at the man.

"Do I know you?" she half shouts for the benefit of those within earshot. "What a ridiculous thing to say to me. My boyfriend brought me here, and I'll thank you to let go of my arm. I'm not underage. I can walk through the bar if I like with no interference from you!"

Having set the scene, she breaks from his grip and bounds through the French doors into the dining room. *That corner table—I'll head for it again.* She dares not look back as she forces her way into a crowd of people filling the space between her and the table. Her brain is numb. In working her way forward, she senses people swirling into the space she vacates—she is walking through dancers—but so what? Is the man still watching from the French doors?

Drop your eyes, Mugs. Stay on course. You're not safe yet.

As she passes between the tables on the far side of the dance floor, tantalizing dinners with courgette Parmesan and a sprig of parsley cupping a cherry tomato pass through her line of vision. They strain her every instinct to grab someone's filet and make a run for it.

You're supposed to be an actress, and you don't even know if you can keep this show on the road, runs through her head.

She glances back at the French doors. The pimp has not moved. He is waiting to see which party she is with. She will have to go on with the act. If she doesn't score soon, she will faint dead away.

"Pardon me, ma'am." A gentleman in a dark suit steps in front of her. Hallelujah! She smiles.

"I've been watching you for a long time, Miss. Your pimp may have the upper hand in the bar, but trolling my dining room is out. I saw you two scheming in the hall."

Margot's head and shoulders slump. *Now it's the manager labelling you. You're dead meat—but you can act, Mugs. Go ahead, act your way out of this one. Lie to him!*

"I beg your pardon! That man in the hall is no friend of mine, and I told him so. If you'll just let me pass, I'll join my party."

"In that case, ma'am, I'll escort you to your table. Please lead the way."

Trapped into continuing the act, she steps by him and walks toward the corner table that she chose when she first arrived. She doesn't have enough energy left to be convincing. Her dad was right. Dreams can't survive on an empty belly.

The manager does not leave her shoulder.

Halfway there, a man takes over her table. *Where did he come from? He doesn't even fit the scene, sitting there in his tieless black shirt and ponytail. What kind of a statement is he trying to make with his New Age hippie-style outfit in a place like this? And he's ruined my next line. How can I say my date is still checking my wrap with* him *sitting there? Buy some time. You'll think of something, Mugs.*

Casually she scoops three peanuts from the bowl on the next table to attract the attention of the two men hunched over their martinis. Not even a glance as they continue to talk of stocks and bonds. She should have taken all the peanuts and bolted.

The corner table and the hippie are only three feet away. *He's drinking ginger ale? No wonder he's sitting in an obscure corner. He's pretending, just like me. Likely a drama student watching the sights. I'll get no dinner out of him. He's as broke as I am.*

Margot's courage begins to break down. She is a lousy actress. She hasn't fooled one of them. Well, maybe the pimp, which is no compliment. She's a failure. Her belly has won. Tomorrow she must go home to Thorsby and let them laugh or else jump off the Burrard Bridge. She'll decide in the morning, depending on which will take less guts. In her vapid state she wonders idly which choice will be the easier.

The manager is speaking to the back of her head.

"I'm sorry I misjudged you, ma'am. I see now that the gentleman at the corner table is expecting you. Please accept my apologies."

Apologies? Because of the neo-hippie? She is so close to fainting that she hasn't noticed the man rise and wave off the manager.

"Hi, there," he says.

It is indeed the man with the ponytail talking to her. She stares his way.

"Yes, you. Please join me. Maybe we can share a plate of chips. You look like you could use something."

Her cover is safe. She might as well sit. Half a plate of chips is better than three peanuts. The man is speaking again.

"You don't belong in here with all these fat-cat business men. You belong on stage."

Some line! *You'd think he could do better than that,* Margot thinks, but she sits. She is past choosing between soup and bus fare. Her head is swimming.

"I'm Ward. What's your name?"

"What's it matter? You read me like a book. Just call me Mary from Hicksville."

"Hey don't be like that. I've been watching you ever since you arrived. It's not by accident that I'm sitting at *your* table. You know, the one you chose when you first came in. I've been enjoying your act and manoeuvring myself toward this moment when we'd meet. You're great!"

Margot is too weak to listen. She wishes he'd order the chips and quit talking, but maybe listening is the price of the chips. Even if her eyes are blurring she needs to listen for her next cue. She turns her head toward the face across the table, but the dance music is louder than the earlier dinner music, and her ears don't seem to be functioning. She wonders what he's saying.

"I came in here to observe these guys. I need to know how businessmen act for the movie I'm making. Then you arrived. What a bonus! You came across that floor with all the creativity of a star."

Margot feels her head sloping to the right. She straightens up and tries to look like she is listening, even though her brain is numb. His lips are still forming words.

"Yes, a star. It's my business to notice. You put on a great show. With your body language and the way you tongue-whipped that pimp in the hall, I can put you in a film any day."

The spinning in her brain swirls to a halt. A job? Is he offering her a job? Margot focuses her eyes. There are no chips on the table. She is hallucinating. Why is he grinning at her?

The kaleidoscope lights of the dance floor are turning her world on end. She wants to rest her head on the table and die.

"Come on, Mary. You can quit the act anytime now. I'm sold. You're great. Here's my card. Come and see me in the morning, and we'll talk about a contract."

Margot stares at him, transfixed. He is playing some form of cruel joke on her. Where are the chips?

"I've found myself a star, Mary. What more can I say to convince you?"

"Margot. My name is Margot."

It doesn't matter if he is offering her a job or putting her on, he's too late. She'd die from starvation before morning. She tries ESP—*Chips, you forgot the chips*—but nothing registers on his face. Her message is too weak.

She can see the outline of his head. Is it leaning her way, or is he rising to leave? It is so hard to focus.

"Good Lord, Margot, can't you hear me? You'll have a contract—your name in lights, all the things you've worked for—you'll be a star!" With each additional phrase, the timbre in Ward's voice increases as he realizes Margot is no longer acting. She's has followed her dreams to near starvation.

He marvels at her poise, seated there stoically trying to carry on, her sequins twinkling, her head swaying gently with the music, a picture to behold if anyone in the dining room had cared to notice. She is indeed a trouper.

He moves to her side and brushes the golden curls on her temple to rouse her, then gently asks, "Shall we celebrate over dinner?"

X

WINNING ROUND ONE

The boy allowed the deliberate push. He offered a smile as his ebony eyes pierced the distance separating him from his assailant. With a quick toss of his head, he flicked his black hair away from his eyes, ever turning to watch his attacker circle for the first punch. He seemed to know that a fight was inevitable.

Around them, children chased across the school playground under the autumn sun and kicked through the crisp leaves that eddied over the fading grass.

A judo kick flashed, followed by three quick punches, all of them meanspirited—sure to blacken an eye or bloody a nose. The smaller boy could not dodge them all.

"Fight! Fight," the school kids hollered as they jostled one another into a ring around the action. Within seconds, every child on the playground crowded in to watch.

The bully's fists shot like pistons, thudding on flesh and bone, yet the younger boy never once retaliated. He just stood there, fists warding off blows when he could, and took the beating.

A second kick was so vicious that instinct caused me to interrupt my walk and move closer to the children.

From the expletives of the bully it became obvious that his victim was new to the school—a boy to be hounded and put down because he was a foreigner.

Aggravated by the courageous manner of the young fellow, the bully hit harder. He needed to see submissiveness, yet his best punch had not removed the new boy's smile or caused him to beg for mercy despite the blood that smeared his upper lip. I had seen that faint smile before in the Middle East and India when boys were fighting. When faced with adversity, it was not in their culture to give in, but why did the boy not fight back?

Some of the children cheered on the bully, thirsting for violence, but most stood quietly, condoning the fight by their silence. If I made no attempt to stop the beating, I would be no different than the silent children. I moved to intervene.

As I approached, a teenager joined the ring—perhaps, judging from his appearance, the little fellow's older brother.

"How's it going, Loni?" he called out.

How's it going? I echoed to myself. *Can't you see the blood-spattered shirt and the swollen lips! About all the boy is managing to do is absorb the pain, and yet you ask, "How's it going?"*

"Great, Idal," the boy shouted with a bloody, lopsided grin. "Meet my new friend, Walter." He indicated the school bully by a nod of his head, for his fists were still raised to ward off numbing blows.

To my surprise, the teenager stopped at the edge of the ring, feet solidly braced apart, arms locked across his chest, as if willing the brawl to continue.

His coal-black eyes missed nothing. His face offered a passive smile the same as Loni's. Like the crowd, I was mesmerized. I watched and waited.

Then came a hush. The thudding blows stopped. All the fight seemed to drain from Walter's spine. He cuffed the new kid playfully on the chest, linked arms with him and walked him from the circle.

"Yeah, I wuz just kiddin' around. We're friends," Walter called back over his shoulder.

XI

UNTITLED NOVEL

In the darkness of early evening, Kate and Harry walk along the beach, side by side, wending their way through scattered boulders, hands thrust deep into pockets. Black cloud boils overhead. Sheer cliffs behind the sand echo the roar of the pounding sea. Harry kicks at a rock, then starts to speak.

"Kate, I'm leaving town." This halts their walking. Harry turns to face the woman. She does not turn his way. With her silence, Harry continues.

"Marrying you would have brought social status, money—a big boost in my career—but I can't do it. I've tried to convince myself for three months that love doesn't matter, but it does. I just can't find passion for someone who acts like a spoiled child, someone who has never accepted 'no' for an answer to anything."

Kate stands staring at the sand. The wind off the sea blows her auburn hair. Harry's words seem to have changed her into a wax doll. She says nothing. Harry waits. Still nothing. He turns and walks ahead.

Tiffany pauses, her hands poised over the keyboard, while she reads the words she has caused to appear on the computer screen—the beginning of her next novel, as yet untitled. The words do not resemble her romance novels, but she feels compelled to go on, and again her nimble fingers tap at the keys.

Through the gloom that paints everything in shades of grey, Kate watches him go, resentment rising inside her—watches and despises every motion of his body, watches the leading edge of tumbling waves come ever closer to his feet before receding. High tide will soon be upon them. She knows they must leave the beach or be washed away. She sees him sit on a boulder, facing away from her, as if waiting for her to catch up so that he can complete the final formality of walking her back to her parents' seaside estate.

Kate does not disguise her approach.

"Harry?" she says softly.

Elbows on knees, he lowers his face into his upturned hands and waits for her to speak again. She smashes his skull with a ten-inch boulder. With arms outflung, he crumples to the sand with the back of his skull crushed like the shell of a Christmas walnut.

The sea nibbles at his fingers as she walks on.

Again, Tiffany scrolls down the screen of her computer. She starts at the beginning of her new novel, as yet untitled, reads to the end, and sits quietly as if waiting for her fingers to continue the story. It's a new kind of story—not like her usual romance novels. Her fingers add "He will not say 'no' again" but stop their typing as if unable to type more.

The doorbell rings. She does not rise. Someone pounds on the door, demanding entry. Tiffany moves the computer mouse to "find and replace" and punches in "Kate," to be replaced with "Tiffany." More pounding on the door. She knows it will be the police. Someone must have found the body before the final surge of high tide.

XII

GREAT NEIGHBOURS

"George, when you finish setting up the card tables, would you pull up the zipper on the back of my dress?"

"Sure, Bessie, but I'll be a few minutes; one of the table legs is sticking."

"Fine, Mr. Fix-it Man. I'll be in the kitchen adding the vodka to the punch."

Knock, knock, knock!

"Now who can that be knocking on the back door at this time of night?" Bessie mumbles. "George, someone's knocking on the back door. It's so dark out there, you come and answer it."

"It's likely a couple of my scouts. They have a project in the basement. I told them they could come over any evening—told them tonight would be fine, that we'd be home playing bridge with our neighbours. I said, 'Always knock three times and let yourselves in.' Unlock the door for them; they won't bother our bridge party, and anyway, I'm busy fixing this table leg."

Mmmm, thinks Bessie, *I can't let them see me with my dress flapping off my shoulders. I'll turn the light on for the basement stairs, unlock the door, and start it opening with the kitchen door closing and go to fix my makeup.*

✑

"Table's fixed, Bessie. I'm here to zip you up," says George. George always makes a big production of all the little things he does around the house. He drops his hands in dismay. "Dear god, Bessie, do you know that the zipper stitching's not holding for a couple of inches at your waistline?"

"It isn't? The guests will be here any minute. I haven't time to change. I'll put that white silk scarf around my waist. That should hide the split."

The doorbell rings.

"Jane, Casey, come in, come in," says George. "I haven't seen you since bridge last spring, and here's Clara right behind you."

George remembers Clara's hair as being white like his own, but tonight Clara's hair is dyed carrot red.

"Hello, George," says Clara. "My husband's out of town, so I made up the fourth with Father O'Malley. Father, meet George, my neighbour." She continues in a joking manner. "The Father makes a safe date, don't you think, George? One never knows who's spying on you, ready to start gossip." Clara laughs as she slaps her bridge partner on the back. George notices that Father O'Malley's deadpan face hasn't cracked a smile and wonders what will happen if he's dealt four aces.

Soon Ed and Dora arrive, and the games of bridge begin. Bessie serves everyone a large glass of punch.

❦

"Tha's mighty fine punch, Bessie," says Dora when the players change tables. "You mus' 'ave more in the kitchen; why not bring it in here so we can, er, um, use it up. Jus' put it on the table and I'll pour for the firs' hour."

After two more hands of bridge, Jane slaps her cards down on the table. "The cards are rotten tonight," she complains. "Let's just visit. We've hardly seen each other during the summer, and we have all winter to play bridge. You're next to the pitcher of punch, Father O'Malley. Why not fill our glasses, and then we'll just visit."

"Good idea," says Ed, settling down on the far side of a card table. "You guys talk, and I'll play solitaire."

"Even better, le's sing," Casey says in a voice that comes out too loud.

"Shh, Casey. Not so loud," whispers his wife, Jane. "And she said talk, not sing."

"Yeah, Bessie," calls out Casey. "Sit yerself down on the pianer shtool and play us a tune. My wife, Jane, jus' told me that she's ready for a good loud singsong! Ain't that right, Jane." Jane scowls at Casey.

Bessie takes her place at the piano, opens the old "Canada Sings" songbook, and hits a chord for "Casey would waltz with a strawberry blonde."

"Great choice of song, Bessie," shouts Casey. "An' the band played on," he joins in with gusto. Soon chairs are pulled into a semicircle around the piano and everyone is singing, everyone but Ed; it interferes with his focus on his game of solitaire.

"Take me out to the ballgame," is in full swing when— *Flap, flap.* "Eeeeeee!" Dora screams.

Bessie collapses backwards off the piano stool. She lands on her back. Her head flops to her chest, then snaps back with a hollow thud as it hits the floor like a pumpkin being dropped from a short height.

Everyone gasps; everyone but Ed, that is. All eyes turn to fixate on the piano. There, spread-eagle across the songbook, clutching to the top edge of it with its little toes, is a big black bat.

Ed calls out, not missing a single play in his game of solitaire, "For that bat to be there, right in front of Bessie's face, its wings must have grazed across her face as it came in for a landing."

"Eeeeeee," Dora continues her scream as she jumps to her feet and flits away down the hall. The bedroom door slams shut.

"Bessie's out cold!" wails Clara as she adjusts Bessie's skirt to show less leg. "Do something, George!"

"Why me? I'm trying to pick up the songbook and get the damn bat out of here before Dora runs into the next county." George, attempting to be the strong scoutmaster, leaves with the songbook held delicately open to encourage the bat to stay put and not flap into his face.

Clara turns to her bridge partner. "Then you do something, Father!"

"Me? You want me to do something?" He sways over to Bessie and absently makes the sign of the cross and starts performing the last rites.

"She's not dead, you idiot; she hit her head when she fell. Didn't you see what happened?"

Father O'Malley looks heavenward for guidance to this question.

"Casey, you used to be a cop. You must know first aid; you look after Bessie," says Clara.

"Yes, Casey. Make yourself useful," snaps his wife, Jane.

"Well," says Casey, "the floor looks kinda hard. She'd be more comfortable on the carpet with that *thick* underlay that George is always bragging about."

"Hey, Ed," Casey calls. "Come an' help me pull Bessie onto the carpet. They don't say two-ton Bessie fer nuthin."

"I'm busy," comes Ed's reply.

"You're not busy; you're jus' playin' solitaire," Casey chastises Ed.

"Yep, but I'm getting some really good moves, so I can't leave *now.*"

Casey swings Bessie, using her bottom as a pivot, and rests Bessie's head on the carpet.

"My hand got bloody!" cries Casey. "She must have a smashed spot on the back of her head hiding in her hair." He rolls her over. Her arms and legs flop with the roll. "Jane, hold my hanky on this bloody spot, and I'll tie the hanky in place with that white belt Bessie's wearing." He yanks off the white scarf that Bessie had tied around her waist. The zipper stitching on the back of Bessie's gown gapes fifteen inches longer than before. Clara snickers. She wondered why Bessie had added a white scarf to that outfit.

"That's not a belt," snaps Casey's wife, Jane. "It's a sash."

"Jeez, Jane, we have an emergency goin' on here, and you're picky about semantics! Just get down here and hold the damn hanky in place."

Purple suffuses Jane's face. "Ask Clara," she bites the words off. "You know I can't bend that low, and I won't stand for your foul language."

Casey and Clara finish tying the sash on the wound.

George returns from the back door white as a sheet. "It flapped at me!" George wails. "Bessie'll have to find her songbook out there in the backyard." He flops into the overstuffed chair, all done in, but raises his head to look down at his wife with her bandaged head.

"Hey, Bessie bled on my Persian carpet. Don't you dare put her on the sofa and bloody it too. She'll wake up just as fast on the floor." He notices Bessie's girdle peaking out through the extended zipper opening. Mortified, his head flops back against the padding of the chair, totally in shock.

Bang, bang, bang! The racket sounds like someone kicking down a door. Two scouts rush up from the basement. One turns to his scoutmaster, as if reporting in. "Sir, you might have a bat in your basement. We thought we heard something flap past us as we went downstairs when we came in." George sits white and unresponsive. The banging continues.

"What's wrong?" the other scout shouts above the din of banging, ready to be the dutiful scout as he stares at Bessie on the floor.

"What's wrong?" Dora yells like a screech owl from the bedroom. "What's wrong is that the bedroom door must have locked when I slammed it shut and not one of you bums came to let me out. That's what's wrong!"

No one moves to help the damsel in distress.

The scouts look quizzically at the silent priest, the man with bloody hands, the fat haughty gal, the fat one with dyed hair, the bandaged form on the floor with ripped clothing showing her girdle, their comatose scout leader, and the guy playing solitaire. One scout catches his friend's sleeve and whispers, "What kind of a game is bridge?"

94

With a shrug and a tiny jerk of his head to suggest it's time they leave, the scout says to the group, "You might try calling 9–1-1."

XIII

THE GREAT WHITE WOLF

From their kitchen window Laura gazes over the foothills of Alberta as she rinses the breakfast dishes. In this household are Walter, his wife, Laura, and their old cat, Smoky.

"Walter, look! A huge albino wolf is running through the tall grass with great leaps. Oh, Walter, he's magnificent; come and look."

"Hmff. I don't see anything moving out there. You're imagining things, Laura. I know that wild animals are working their way into the city, but I don't think you'll find a wolf this near the suburbs, even if we are on the outskirts of the city."

Laura removes her apron, checks on old Smoky, the cat, and leaves with Walter for work.

⌘

The next morning Laura thinks she sees the white wolf again but doesn't mention it to Walter. *No need for him to think I'm going dotty,* she says to herself. *The wolf looks rather wispy anyway and is moving slower, moving as if he is waiting for something to happen. Maybe he's hunting—looking for easy prey. We must keep Smoky in the house; he's so old and slow he wouldn't have a chance against the power of that beautiful beast.*

Like every other morning, Walter puts the garbage out back and waits for Laura in the front hall. She hangs up her apron, checks that Smoky is sleeping in the basket by their bed, and leaves with Walter.

The following day, at the sink, she calls, "Walter, come quickly; you'll see the white wolf this time. He's poised to jump over our fence!" Laura rushes to the TV room's sliding doors for a better view. She sees Smoky running in the garden— running towards the wolf.

"Walter! The wolf is going to get Smoky!" Before her eyes she sees the wolf stand on his back legs with human shoulders and arms that gently lift Smoky to cuddle him. Then the view fades, and Laura bursts into tears.

"The wolf caught Smoky," she cries. "You were here in time to see it happen, Walter. You must have seen him this time."

"I was here, but I didn't see any wolf. I'm sure you'll find Smoky in his basket by our bed. Come; let's look." Sure enough, Smoky lies curled up on his blanket, but he doesn't raise an eyebrow or flick his tail in recognition of their attention. Walter leans over to stroke the cat. His hand touches the soft fur and quickly recoils.

"Laura, my dear Laura," he cries. "Smoky is limp. He rubbed against my legs this morning, but I do believe he has passed away." Walter pauses. "I'm glad he had a painless passing." They hold each other and cry. Walter cries for the passing of their loving family member. Laura sobs for what she had seen in the garden. She wonders if the great white wolf was a vision she alone saw—a vision of how all beloved family pets pass on with grace and dignity.

XIV

UNDERSTANDING PEOPLE – A PERSONAL ESSAY

You can understand some people, and others are unfathomable. Take my sons, for instance. I can understand them when it comes to me driving our outboard motorboat. The boys are in their fifties, and I'm in my eighties. Our cottage is on an island, and I've been driving that seventeen-foot boat, or one like it, for fifty-nine years, like when they were kiddies all done up in their little life jackets trusting me to run the boat safely. Sometimes, I have a week at the cottage when none of the family members are at the lake, so why shouldn't I turn the key in the boat's dashboard and take off for town to buy groceries? At thirty miles an hour it only takes a few minutes. Granted that sometimes the first five minutes can be consumed working on the mooring knots when the ropes are wet, but I keep a screwdriver handy, and once I've skewered the knots a few times they come undone before I have to stand up to rest my legs. And I can't exactly just "turn the key" and take off. My fingers are too weak to turn the key; it's pretty stiff, but I keep a pair of pliers on the dashboard of the boat. I pinch the key with the pliers, aim at the keyhole, twist, and the motor turns over just fine. Because my boys love me and don't want any harm to come to me, they merely suggest that maybe I should go for groceries with the neighbours.

You see? I understand my boys quite well. They sometimes call me "Miss Independence," maybe too independent for their liking, but they know better than to say I can't go. They don't want me to feel *guilty* when I take the boat out anyway—against their good advice.

I'm a fish in water—swim better than I can walk. With this boat's broad beam it's not like it's going to capsize or sink, even in a storm, and it's not as if the route to town is empty of traffic. Why, there are boats going into town and home again all the time. If I were to run into trouble, I'd just put on my dumb old lady look, and someone would come to my assistance.

My boys know it's not likely that I'd fall overboard and drown, and they also know that to stop driving the boat would dash my love of the lake. They suggest groceries with the neighbours just to show me that they care. After all, if you live alone on an island, even with neighbours, you need a boat just in case you have to use it—a boat all gassed up and ready to go.

Yes, I understand my boys' thoughts very well. They suggest the "riding with the neighbours" story just to leave the door open for me to run the boat while they hope that nothing goes wrong.

This summer I took the boat one day on just such a trip when none of the family were down. It was a fine day with a bit of a west wind. Where I wanted to park the boat, a west wind would be to my advantage in catching the dock. I think about this because my weak fingers don't catch a dock very well. So off I went—out past the point and around towards a small island that marks that part of the lake where you swing off to the right to head into the bay where the town wharfs are located or go straight ahead into a nearly empty bay. This bay has a business block on the left shore and some private docks and a mini gas marina on the right shore just as you first enter the bay.

I had to go to town that day for a lawyer's appointment, so I went straight ahead and tied up at their wharf on the left. The lawyer's appointment went well, but on the way home, fifty feet from the dock, the motor conked out.

Out of gas, I figured—time to put the hose over to the other tank. My fingers were still strong enough to do that job—maybe a bit slowly, mind you, but finally I was ready to start up again. The west wind had carried the boat a bit down that empty bay, but the motor would finish off that distance pretty quickly.

Thread the key into the pliers and give it a twist and off we'll go. But it didn't take off. No matter what I did, the motor wouldn't start. I had a plan for that—my cellphone.

I soon discovered that cellphones aren't much use if you haven't loaded them with local phone numbers. The only number I knew was for the cottage, and there was no one there. Not to worry; 4–1-1 should work in this town.

I asked to be connected to the mini marina just across the bay near the private docks. I figured that they could help me out. The 4–1-1 operator called the number for me.

Three rings, and they answered. The gas docks employ high school kids in the summer to handle the gas sales. I explained that I was the green boat floating in the middle of the bay and asked them to please come and tow me in.

"Hold on for a second," she says. Well, her idea of a second and mine weren't the same, because she came back about five minutes later and said in a cheery, upbeat voice, "I can't find the manager, and we can't take the boat out without his permission, so I guess we can't help. G'bye."

With that she hung up before I could say a word, and there I was, floating east towards the end of the bay pretty fast in that west wind.

I looked for boats on the water, and they all swung off to the right and headed into town. No one came towards the private docks across from me or left them.

"So I'm stuck out here," sez I to myself. "I'll just get out my old paddle and paddle over to the gas dock. I didn't take canoe lessons in my youth for nothing. I know how to make a C stroke and a J stroke."

I sat back on the port side gunwale and paddled a good strong stroke. Actually, it felt great to be paddling, with the summer sun glinting on the water and the wind in my hair, even if it was that troublesome wind blowing me east.

Now and then I checked the shoreline to see how I was getting on. The wind on my broadside blew me down into the boot of the bay faster than I could move forward. Well, I could fix that. With a few C strokes I brought the bow around so the wind would glance off the bow and canvas top of my boat, like on a sail of a sailboat, and thus add to my forward momentum like beating upwind. This helped, but I still floated east in the wind faster than my headway across the bay.

I paddled and I paddled. The thought crossed my mind that old ladies don't paddle seventeen-foot boats. It might not be good for my health. I checked to see if I was puffing or if I felt faint. No, I felt fine, so I kept on paddling.

When I checked again on the shoreline the boulders that formed the foot of the bay were much nearer—well, right beside me. At this close range, about five feet away, I could determine the speed of my forward motion, boulder by boulder, with each stroke. *Really,* thinks I, *I'm still a pretty good paddler,* and I struck out with even more vigour to prevent the stern and motor propeller from scraping on the rocks. Then thinks I, *There's something wrong here; I should be getting tired. Adrenalin—I wonder if that's been keeping me going! I wonder if it can run out!*

By now with the wind pushing me east, I'd circled right around inside the whole end of the bay, about ten times the original distance I'd contemplated. My strokes now carried me back up the other side of the bay. From the breeze, I judged that the wind had died a bit. *Whoop-de-doo, I'm going to win this battle after all.* I figured that the town buildings sheltered this side of the bay and this lee side allowed me to go faster. I was amazed that in all this time, about forty minutes, I hadn't seen one boat near those private docks. Another ten minutes and I should be up to the docks where I could tie up, if I could find an open spot and walk for help. So on I paddled.

As I neared the private docks, I saw the small twelve-passenger catamaran ferry boat leaving the nearest private dock. *Good. I can tie up in its spot.* On second glance, the catamaran seemed to be coming my way. The driver called out, "Do you need some help, lady?"

Need he ask? I sez to myself—a white-haired old woman paddling a seventeen-footer! I smiled and said I was glad to see him. I took out our tow rope and tied a firm sailor's sheet bend to my bow line, and he towed me back the fifteen feet to his dock.

"Yep" he said when we had tied up. "I been watching ya fer some time now and wondered why a white-haired ol' gal would be paddlin' against that wind."

Why indeed! Now him, I didn't understand. If he'd been watching and thinking about helping me, why didn't he think a little faster? Then in a good-natured way he insisted on towing me all the way back to my cottage where all the neighbours would see our arrival and tell my sons that I'd had trouble. But my boys, they're sweethearts. If they heard about my escapade, they didn't say a word, and I'm still driving the boat when I'm alone at the lake. The boys and I understand each other perfectly, but that catamaran operator, *him* I don't understand! Offering to help after he'd been sitting there, watching me paddle and paddle and paddle.

XV

FREEMAN RIVER

Wilderness! Miles and miles of wilderness! Even the word sounds unpredictable, thought Greg as he sat with his heels digging into the pebbled beach, his back against a gnarled tree. He wondered why a city kid like him would find the wilderness so magical. *Beauty? Adventure? Danger? All true,* he mused as he toyed with the significance of each word and considered the scene before him.

A warm breeze ruffled the bulrushes growing in the shallows, birds whistled, and the sun hung in the evening sky. He felt at peace. His gaze spread to the bend in the river where mountain water rippled on its way to the prairies. The distant hills and sky blended to form a backdrop for the willows and dogwoods growing along the far bank.

This was Greg's first summer job away from home. It had brought him to the oil fields of Swan Hills, Alberta. The work camp's portable trailers nestled among the trees along the Freeman River, and all around the tracts of spruce forest filled the horizon. The workers ventured into the forests on their days off, and by midsummer they had climbed every height and explored each glistening lake. When no one was available for a ramble, Greg would go down to the river. It wasn't that far from the bunkhouse, and it was a great spot for fishing.

"Hey, Greg! Come and have a beer with the new guy who just arrived! We're having our usual welcome party."

Greg roused from his thoughts and realized that dusk had finally settled. He looked at his watch: ten thirty! Northern latitudes really lengthened a day.

As Greg climbed the path to the bunkhouse a shaft of light from the open door filtered through the darkened trees.

"Give us a hand with the new guy's canoe, Greg," called someone.

They stashed the boat in the bushes and carried the paddles into the bright lights and laughter of the party, which was getting underway.

"Meet the new man; this here's Mel. It looks like he does his hiking by canoe," said Hank, the self-appointed master of ceremonies, raising his beer can in a welcome.

"It's good to be back, fellas," said Mel, in acknowledgment of their hospitality. "When I worked in Swan Hills five years back, my buddies and I used to paddle old Beulah down to the Crossroads all the time. You ought to try it."

As conversation wound down, Mel spoke up once more: "I meant it, fellas. If any of you want to take my canoe out on the river, just leave a note on my bed and take the blades out of the closet. It's fine with me."

❧

The next day Greg took his fishing rod down to the river to practice casting with some new flies.

"How ya doin', Greg," said Mel as he came down the path. "On a nice night like this you should have tried out the canoe. I meant what I said about using it if you want to."

Greg enjoyed canoeing, so they talked about making a trip down the Freeman River.

"You'll need two cars and about three hours for the run, so give yourself plenty of time to be out before the sun goes down."

"If it's nice, we could try tomorrow," Greg suggested.

"Go ahead, but find someone else. I'm busy."

Later that evening Greg checked with another summer student, a wiry redhead named Johnny.

"Yeah, we can do it tomorrow, as long as you know where you're going, because I sure don't." Johnny laughed. They agreed to meet when they finished work at four o'clock.

"Cookie, we'll be ready to leave at five o'clock. Any chance for an early supper for Johnny and me? It doesn't have to be hot, just something fast."

"Sure thing, Greg. If it's not enough, I'll leave you something for later."

Greg and Johnny changed into jeans and T-shirts and drove tandem down to well site 16. They headed through the bush, following the ruts that led to a gravel shingle stretching out into the river known locally as the Crossroads. They dropped off one car, returned to camp, ate, and hurried down to the river with the canoe on their shoulders, quite pleased at getting away before five thirty.

"You paddle the stern, Greg; I don't know much about a canoe," said Johnny as he climbed in from dry land and crept forward to the bow rather than getting his feet wet. Greg rolled his pants, put his runners and socks in the canoe, and waded into the water to free the boat from shore.

The sun warmed Greg's back as they slipped along easily with the current.

"Do you see that—in that little bay?" Johnny asked, pointing with his paddle. "There goes a mallard duck finning along with her brood."

"Look how clear the water is," observed Greg, resting his paddle across the gunwales for a moment to still the water." You can see the rocks on the bottom with minnows darting in and out of the reeds."

Just then Johnny's paddle scraped bottom. He watched carefully from the bow as Greg steered them around the rocks, but soon the water depth was too shallow for the safety of the boat.

"This is hopeless, Johnny. We're going to ruin the bottom of the canoe if we keep this up. I guess the river is lower than Mel figured. With just getting back here, he wouldn't recognize how little it's rained. Maybe if we get out and walk, we can float the canoe along until we get past these rapids."

Greg rolled his jeans higher and stepped into the icy water. Johnny managed to keep his balance, even though his runners slipped on the slimy moss covered rocks.

"Ouch! This is murder on my feet," Greg hollered. "Hold on a minute while I put my runners back on."

"Got a match, Greg? Mine just fell in the water."

"Nope. I don't smoke."

Slowly they worked their way downstream, pushing the canoe along between them until they passed the rapids and came to deeper water. With sodden shoes they climbed back into the canoe and continued downstream, enjoying the profusion of nature. The sun remained high in the evening sky, spilling its warm yellow glow along the banks of the river.

"Look at those, would you!" Johnny exclaimed as they came upon some peculiar stick mounds extending into the river.

"They're beaver lodges. If we round this next bend very quietly, we might see a beaver working on his dam."

"Are you trying to tell me that we found deep water because we're going to come up against a beaver dam downstream?" cried Johnny.

"Likely, but it won't be hard to get the canoe past it. We'll beach the canoe and carry it around on shore."

They dipped their blades with the stealth of a native war party and glided around the next bend in the river to see if they could sneak up on any unsuspecting beavers.

"Hi there," came a voice from a small punt with two fishermen. "Great day for fishing."

The boys were so surprised to find other people in such an out-of-the-way place, they were speechless for a moment, and it showed on their faces.

"You've come across our favourite fishin' hole," said one of the men with a smile. "We come here all the time with our bush buggy from the Crossroads and camp just over there," he added, pointing out a battered vehicle parked by an orange two-man tent on the far shore. The men had been there two days and were about to drive back to Fort Assiniboine. Greg and Johnny said their goodbyes and headed downstream.

"Hey, fellas," Johnny shouted back to the men. "Have you got any matches?" They gave Johnny a light and waved away the extended hand when he tried to return the half-used matchbook.

"Keep 'em. You'll want another smoke before you're finished." The boys said their thanks and continued their journey down the river. With all their talking, there wasn't a beaver to be seen, but the beavers' destruction was overwhelming. The dammed river had overflowed its banks and spilled into low areas, making lagoons no better than swamp. Bushes and trees trapped in the water were dying, and everywhere were the gnawed stumps of young trees.

"There's the beaver dam ahead," Greg said. "Can you see a low spot where there's a spillway? Maybe we can slip right over."

The dam was a big one! They moved towards the shore, but with water spilling into the forest, the shore was nonexistent. In disgust, they climbed out of the canoe and worked it over the watery sticks and mud. Downstream the river slowed to a trickle. They pushed on as before, floating the canoe in ankle-deep water, as they sloshed over the rock strewn riverbed. Greg's jeans wouldn't stay rolled and bit by bit became wet like Johnny's.

In some places they had to carry the canoe on their shoulders, hooding their vision. Trying to keep it balanced as they constantly slipped on slimy rocks and moss was exhausting. The fading sun slipped lower in the sky as they plodded along in silence.

"I was just thinking, Johnny. We're taking a chance walking along here this time of night. My mom trains scout leaders, and she says you have to keep talking. If you startle a bear by walking in silence, you may cross between her and her cub, and she might attack. If you make lots of noise as you walk, she'll hear you, find a hiding place, and watch you go by. My kid brother has a little bell attached to his backpack."

Greg could sense that his own apprehension was making a long story of it, just to keep talking. Now and then they came to parts of the river deep enough to continue paddling.

Each time, they hoped the water would last, and sometimes it did for several bends.

"Damn! Time to walk again. I didn't expect all these rocks," Johnny complained. On they trudged, their runners aspirating loud enough to kill the silence as the water sucked in and out with each step.

It's eight thirty; our three hours are up," said Johnny, trying to mask the anxiety in his voice. "How much farther do you think it will be to the Crossroads?"

"I dunno," Greg answered, unsure of their location. "The river has caused us to lose some time, but we haven't stopped. I'd say by nine, nine thirty, we should make it."

An eerie cry split the air.

"My god! What was that?" shrieked Johnny.

"Don't worry! That's a good sign. It's a loon. If there's a loon around here, there must be deep water." Just then Johnny stumbled. He rolled over, sitting in four inches of water, thoroughly soaked, and slapped its surface in a silent oath. "As if I weren't wet enough," he fumed as he regained his footing and took hold of his end of the canoe. "Just listen to those dumb birds, sitting there squawking. I think they're laughing at me."

The commotion had caught the eye of some curious grey jays. Three of them had come to watch the boys and were perched on a nearby branch. Like kids in the booster bleachers at a baseball game, they cheered the boys with raucous enthusiasm.

"You can't be mad at those birds, Johnny," Greg teased, to find a happier frame of mind. "That's the famous grey jay. The locals call them whiskey jacks. They like to be sociable."

As predicted, they found deeper water and were able to climb back into the canoe.

"Where's that loon? I'd like to thank him personally for his private water supply," quipped Johnny.

"Over there, see? There are two of them silhouetted against the setting sun."

"Just what we need, a setting sun," muttered Johnny.

Greg and Johnny rounded one bend after another, each time expecting to see the Crossroads and each time finding more raw nature. The growth of wild roses along the river-bank seemed drained of colour as the lingering twilight lost its intensity, and the air became cooler.

Greg looked at his watch—nine forty-five. *The Crossroads must be quite near,* he thought. *Johnny's paddling quite well for a beginner, strong and rhythmic.* The unending crescendo made by crickets and frogs dulled their senses as their paddles moved—dip, swing, dip, swing, dip, swing, dip, swing.

"Now hear this. Now hear this," Greg's paddle seemed to say to him. *What a ridiculous thing for me to hear from a paddle,* he thought, but still he listened to the mesmerizing rhythmic sound. His mind wandered back to when his moth-er used the old wringer washing machine at the lake and they would play games listening to its motor and hearing words from its constant groaning.

His wet pants and shoes felt like ice packs on his legs and feet. The strength of the wilderness pushed in from every side. He conceded that he was getting tired, but Johnny was plugging on, so he kept up his rhythm and they slipped along in silence.

"Now hear this. Now hear this," Greg's paddle whispered again. His mind shifted back to his mother. She had her ways, and sometimes, to pry any of her four boys from the television, she would plant herself in front of the TV screen and mimic a ship's captain, saying, "Now hear this. Now hear this. This is your mother speaking." Then she would add her important message: "Cut the lawn," "Shovel the snow," or "Who's finished their homework?" This was the first summer he hadn't cut the lawn, Greg mused as he pulled again on his paddle.

"Now hear this. Now hear this," sang Greg's paddle.

Will that crazy thought not leave my head! The last time Mom did that was during the winter, he remembered. What was it she wanted? Oh yes, she was waving a piece of paper at us and saying something about it being the next camping lecture for scout training and we were to read it because it was something we should know, even if we weren't scouts. Then she stood there blocking the TV screen until we had all dutifully read it.

"STOP" was all he could remember from the paper, but his mind kept nagging him. Oh yes, "What to do in an emergency." S for stop, T for think, O for organize and P for plan, or was it "Proceed?" The other side of the paper was all about hypothermia.

His mother's final words resounded in his brain. "You have to learn about it before it happens! You have to know about the circumstances when hypothermia will happen, because once you have the symptoms, your mind won't function well enough to do anything about it. You may not realize you're just plugging ahead like a robot." Adrenalin shot through Greg's body. *Maybe that's why Johnny is so silent and paddling like a mechanical man.*

"Hey, Johnny," Greg spoke into the silence. There was no answer. "*Hey, Johnny,*" He shouted. "*Hey, Johnny, hey Johnny, hey Johnny*" echoed the dark sullen hills around them, until all was quiet again.

"What?" Johnny mumbled.

"What d'ya say, Johnny—you cold, tired? How's it going?"

No answer. Johnny just kept digging with his paddle.

Darn, I wish I had read that paper better, Greg brooded. He started over. "STOP. Stop for emergencies," it had read. *I have to make a decision,* thought Greg. *Even if the Crossroad and my car are just around the corner, we can't take a chance on bumbling down the river in the dark. Hypothermia, Mom called it. She said, "Do something to prevent it before it gets you." If only I could remember! We are tired and hungry, and worst of all we're cold and wet—perfect candidates! Johnny may already be in trouble.*

The sky still seemed light, but the riverbank seemed darker than before. Ten p.m.—half an hour before dark, real dark. Greg steered for shore and crunched the bow onto the gravel beach. Johnny did not move. Greg heard his voice commanding Johnny to get out: "Pick up the canoe! Good! Now go straight ahead to those bushes." Johnny stood there like a zombie, staring into the dark undergrowth, and let the boat slither to the ground.

Greg could see an overhanging mudbank for protection behind the first row of willows. He decided that it might be more out of the wind if they camped between the mudbank and the willows where there was a little rise in the beach. He caught Johnny's elbow and urged him forward to the clearing. *Heat! Gotta have heat,* his mind ordered. "Come on, Johnny, help me get some wood."

There was plenty of dead wood in the bush, but feeling for it in the dark and ripping it free took time—more time than he could spare. Johnny didn't help. Greg gathered as big a pile of wood as he could, while Johnny plunked himself down near the woodpile and shivered as he stared at the ground.

Greg was no Boy Scout, but family outings had taught him a few things, and soon he had a little pile of birch twigs packed around a wad of spruce resin. Greg searched for the matches in Johnny's pockets. Now with darkness, cold started to set in, and his fingers felt stiff. "It's a good thing Johnny smokes and got those matches," he muttered as he lit the first match.

Zztt. The match scratched across the folder and went out. So did the next one.

"Gotta get closer," Greg said aloud. He positioned himself on the windward side of the birch twigs and shielded the operation with his shivering backside to the wind.

Zztt. The match flickered. As he lowered his shaking hands to the branches, the flame snuffed out again. "Cheap matches," Greg growled. He clutched the package in the darkness, felt for a match, and tore away a fourth one. It was all he could do to strike the match as his fingers willfully jerked and floundered in the night air.

Try again. Easy does it. You've only got two left, penetrated his thoughts. *Get down, plant your elbows, and keep those hands still! Do it right. Please, God, help me do it right.* He struck the next match. *Zztt.* The little flame held, and he prayed as he lowered it the one inch to his lump of resin.

Slowly the tension in his body released as the flames spread to the twigs. He fed the spot of light with more twigs and placed bigger branches near the flames until he was sure of success. The heat felt good.

Greg roused Johnny and brought him close to the fire. His watch read 11:00 p.m. The velvet darkness filled every direction except for the flickering on the mudbank and glow from the firelight on their tired faces.

"Jeez, my rear end is cold. This is supposed to be summer!" Greg took off his wet shoes and pushed his feet into the clammy sand, then raised them to the fire. The heat felt good. *Now for the waiting,* he thought.

"Hey, Johnny, have you ever stayed in the bush all night? Johnny, are you listening to me?"

Johnny just shivered and stared at the fire. Greg's adrenalin rose again as he realized that Johnny really was in trouble.

Gotta do something, but what?

"He's cold, but how do I get him warm?" The voice Greg heard was his own, but it seemed to be a comfort. "Come on, Johnny, off with that wet T-shirt," Greg said as he peeled off Johnny's wet shirt and slipped his own dry shirt over Johnny's head and body. *Next comes Johnny's shoes, socks, pants and underwear,* Greg's mind coached. Greg retrieved his dry socks from the boat and pulled them onto Johnny's frigid feet. He removed his pants to get his undershorts for Johnny and pulled on his jeans again. They'd just have to do him until he could dry some of the clothes. He draped them over bushes close to the fire, gathered rocks from the beach, and set them around the fire to heat—rocks a good size for putting in their runners or into the wet socks after they had a bit of time to heat. Next he dragged the canoe up behind Johnny and propped it on its side with rocks to trap heat from the fire between its concave interior and the mudbank.

The thought of going into the bush again, in total darkness, groping his way to search for more wood, seemed insane, but he could see no other way as the fire's ravenous appetite depleted the wood pile. Submissive, Greg tugged on his damp runners and plunged into the forest, his arms up to protect his head and chest from branches. Feeling his way in the dark, he found wood much farther than he had gone before. Each time he went out, the light of the fire was there to guide him back.

Greg slaved on until he collapsed from exhaustion.

The inactivity was chilling. "One thirty. What a lousy way to spend a night!"

Greg built a bigger fire and rested. Only the crackle of the flames and rustling of leaves, as if some animal was in furtive retreat, broke the silence. Johnny felt warm against Greg's bare top as he snuggled down beside his sleeping friend to share his body heat.

Time slipped by as Greg gazed into the fire and watched the flames sink lower and lower as if they were part of a ritual dance that would come to an end. *Dear Lord, I've never been so cold,* seemed to be a prayer going through his head that he couldn't quite grasp.

Cold! With this he came to his senses. "The fire! Can't let it go out," Greg screamed into the darkness and dragged himself over to the woodpile, fully awake again.

"Won't this night ever end?" he cried.

With the fire renewed, Greg checked the clothes bush. Johnny's T-shirt and socks were dry, so he put them on. "Hmm, not my colour scheme, but warm. Ha, at least I have my sense of humour back." He felt Johnny's jeans and repositioned them near the fire.

"Come on, Johnny, wake up and get yourself warmer near the fire." Greg could not make any sense of Johnny's mumbled reply. The shoes were dry. Greg spilled the hot rocks out of them and put on his shoes, then struggled to get Johnny's feet into his shoes. The warm rock his shoes had been sitting on felt good. He cradled it in his hands.

"Wake up, Johnny. Maybe this rock would feel good if you cradled it in your lap." With no response from Johnny, Greg placed several warm rocks around Johnny's legs and in his lap and then built up the fire.

After some time Johnny stirred. "Wha' gives?" he blurted. "Wha's goin' on?"

"Don't you remember?" Greg asked.

Looking around, Johnny ruffled his hair. "I'm cold. Where's m' pants?"

""Drying," Greg answered. The pants were dry, so he tugged them onto his helpless friend.

Johnny dozed again, then roused with a jerk. "Why's it so dark? What time is it?"

"Don't ask. Each hour has ninety minutes," but Johnny wasn't listening. Had he gone to sleep again, or had he passed out? Again Greg's adrenalin surged. Johnny needed help. Greg kept the fire blazing and warmed rocks to pack close to Johnny. He cradled him as they huddled together in the curved backdrop of the canoe to share their body warmth and rest his weary limbs. He watched with despair as the woodpile grew low again. Would it last until sunrise?

Greg watched the black and greys of the forest finally take on colour at 5:00 a.m. The river was shrouded in midst, and upwind Greg could see the dim outline of a deer drinking at the water's edge. Rays of sunlight shone through the mist and warmed his shoulders as he kicked sand over the fire.

Greg dragged himself and the canoe down to shore, and then helped his friend down to the river.

"Wha' happened to our canoe trip?" Johnny wanted to know.

The current was strong. Greg couldn't believe it was the same river that had confounded them the night before. The mist lifted, and the river glistened in all its morning splendour as the current carried them along the first few bends. Greg's watch read 5:45.

"Halloo," Mel bellowed as they came around a bend in the river. "Greg, Johnny, over here, on the bank," he called, motioning for them to cut towards the shore. "Boy, am I glad to see you two guys." He grinned as he caught the bow of the canoe.

"You're a beautiful sight yourself," Greg sighed.

"Let me paddle there, Johnny," Mel said when he saw Johnny more closely and the idle paddle in the bottom of the canoe. "We'll pick up the cars, and I'll radio the company to call off the search party they were getting together for this morning. Then we'll get back to camp and feed you guys," Mel added to encourage them as he set his big shoulders to work.

They paddled towards the Crossroads, content to let Mel continue with his friendly monologue.

"I got your note that you had the boat, Greg. When I realized you were overdue, I notified the company and came out last night to look for you. As soon as I saw the river, I realized it was too low and knew what had happened. I camped by the cars overnight and put a light on shore so you wouldn't pass by in the dark. I hiked out here this morning to see if I could find you. I just hoped there was enough camper in the two of you to survive hypothermia. Older hands than you two have bought it out here in the bush, y'know. You don't get a second chance!"

Greg checked his watch—7:10. Had they tried to keep going last night, it would have been close to one a.m. before they reached the Crossroads. Two or more hours in the dark, cold, and wet and totally exhausted. Mel was right, but they *had* survived. Greg dipped his head in a silent prayer for their deliverance. He wasn't sure what he had done right, but he was determined that before it happened again, he would find out.

About the Author

Lyn Thompson grew up in Winnipeg surrounded by stories from her father, P.M. Abel, the editor of the Country Guide magazine. With her B.Sc. in Human Ecology and a post-graduate in dietetics completed, Lyn married petroleum engineer, Bill Thompson in 1953. After an interesting and exciting life, they retired to Calgary where Lyn continues to live as a widow.

Her background is especially suited to writing short stories, for she delighted in studying people and situations in her childhood as well as in the many locations where they lived – oil towns on Canada's western prairies, and in Peru, United States, The Middle East and England. Some stories are pure fiction while others portray real life situations. The stories in *Patchwork Stories* are based on these experiences and Lyn's imagination. She weaves the knowledge of sports, outdoor lore and volunteerism into her writing, and has held credentials as a Guide and Scout leader, a swimming instructor, scuba diver, first-aider, and wilderness trainer. Sports included golf, downhill skiing, curling, and swimming. Lyn has spent over sixty years enjoying their family cottage and all it has to offer in outdoor life, boating, and family togetherness.

Lyn has actively pursued the craft of writing since 1990. She has coordinated a WGA critique group since that time and served on the Writers' Guild of Alberta executive. In 2008 she was honoured with a WGA Life Membership. Lyn works in several genres but prefers to write short stories, novels, and her own style of poetry.

Her other works include *Hypothermia*, *Outhouse Memories and Other Cottage Poems*, *Bella A Woman of Courage 1863-1953*, and two books of short stories *Blind Justice*, and *Children of the Thirties*.

Visit Lyn at
www.lynthompson.com

CPSIA information can be obtained at www.ICGtesting.com
Printed in the USA
LVOW10s0811161214

418969LV00007B/101/P